Love Me in the End

Love Me in the End

Are perfect matches still made in heaven?

Sonia Kundra Singh

MP

MAHAVEER PUBLISHERS

Published by
MAHAVEER PUBLISHERS
4764/2A, 23-Ansari Road, Daryaganj
New Delhi – 110002
Ph. : 011 – 66629669–79–89
Fax : 011 – 41563419
e-mail : mahaveerpublishers@gmail.com

First Published: March 2011

Love Me in the End
ISBN (10) : 8183520812
ISBN (13) : 9788183520812

Distributed in India by
VAIBHAV BOOK SERVICE
e-mail : vaibhavbookservice@gmail.com

Distributed in Nepal by
BAJRANGBALI BOOK ENTERPRISES PVT. LTD.
Jyatha Mushyabahal, Ward No. 27, Kathmandu, Nepal
e-mail : bajrangbalibooks@gmail.com

Printed by Jaico Printers, New Delhi

Dedications

To Papa and Mama who have always encouraged me to follow my dreams… this is the fruit of their motivation.

Also the driving force of my life who kept my inspiration of the 'perfect' hero alive in my mind… my love, Vaibhav.

For the Team 28 AD and all the army wives out there, it's time for dreams to come true!

Acknowledgement

This book could not have been possible but for my parents who gave me the freedom to lock myself in my room and spend my every waking hour writing! Thank you Papa for all the exciting travels I have had with you. Those experiences were unforgettable and enriched my writing.

Thank you, Vaibhav, for letting me become the writer I am today, by letting me spend timeless hours while you poured over my novel in spite of your busy and rigorous schedule.

Thank you Supriya and Anoop for all your support and helping me create my website that opened a virtual world of opportunities for me!

Also the pillars of my life—Neetu, Jiju and five-year old Shlok (who kept wanting to play games on my laptop, but never could!)

Finally my dearest in-laws who have always shown me unconditional love and encouragement.

I am also grateful to the team of Mahaveer, my publishers, who were very encouraging throughout and particularly Binay Dutt for making things happen for me.

"Maybe if our engagement bothers you so much, then you should tell your Dad, but calmly," he added in the end.

"You tell him."

"I did tell him, remember? In clear words."

"Then?"

"I think he mostly ignores what I say." Arman hid a smile knowing that smile was the last thing Ria wanted him to do.

"Fine!" Ria tried to wriggle out of his hold, but he held on. "Let me go. I think I told you earlier too, not to touch me."

"How do you expect to live with me when we get married?" Arman drawled lazily. "I'm going to touch you all the time then."

Prologue

"You did what?" Lying on the bed, Vidhya Melhera glared helplessly at her husband Amitab before asking, "*Why?*"

"*Shush!*" Taking off his shirt and discarding it carelessly on a nearby chair, Amitab walked towards his wife of thirteen years, "You will wake up the whole house."

"Amitab, if you don't tell me right now what's going on, I swear I *will* wake up the whole house," said Vidhya, her eyes narrowing dramatically and making her face look years younger.

She was beautiful, Amitab Melhera concluded as he pulled the sheets over the bed and slid in, "It was the best thing to do."

"Best thing to do?" Rising up, Vidhya threw her pillow at him, hitting him squarely on his chest. "If you think I'm going to feel happy about it, then think twice Mr Know-it-all."

"You should," Amitab Melhera bantered with an amused smile playing on his lips. "Ria is almost sixteen now and I can't think of a better person for her..."

"It's the twenty-first century Amitab! Girls don't get married when they are sixteen!"

"Vidhya…," Amitab threw the pillow back at her, deliberately hitting her on her breasts. The pillow bounced back enticingly, "I'm *not* getting Ria married; just engaged."

After glaring at him for his argument, Vidhya fell back on the bed, staring glumly at the ceiling. "But, why?" she asked.

"Today's generation," he replied, shrugging helplessly, "I can't trust them any more."

"Are you saying that you don't trust *my* daughter?"

"*Shush*!" he said, resting his head close to her and playing with a few strands of her hair. "*Our* daughter, Vidhya. I know I'm not her father but I do love her more than a real father would as I have seen her grow. How can you forget that?"

Yes, how could she forget that? Vidhya felt a sharp twinge at hurting him. She shouldn't have said that. Amitab might be years older than her but his mind and heart worked just like a child's. Even though it was a second marriage for both, Vidhya knew that she had not loved anyone as she loved Amitab now.

"I'm sorry," she whispered. To Vidhya he did not seem more than thirty years of age, but Amitab Melhera was fifty-two now. Apart from the slight greying at his temples, Amitab could lure a girl of nineteen years right into his bed. Smiling at her silly musings and feeling possessive about her husband, she traced his lips slowly, "But Ria is *so* young…"

"I know. That's why I want to protect her," he said and she believed him. "Already I can see she is at that delicate age where boys…," he grimaced as he continued, "I mean *young* boys are going to bait her and when the time comes, I don't want to stay at home worrying for her…"

"She might choose wisely," Vidhya contradicted quietly.

"Oh…I don't think I want to know what's wise according to her," he teased. "And the person I have chosen for her is very good…he is already working in his father's office and in a few more years, he would be heading the New York office all by himself."

"Don't you believe in love marriages then? It happens you know. Boy meets girl or vice versa and they do fall in love…like we did; take Tanvi and Pratinav," Vidhya voiced slowly. Now both of them were married *and* happy.

Pratinav was Amitab's son from his first wife and Tanvi was her cousin. It was a love match right from the start. And thinking back about Tanvi's old life, where she had been abused by a drunkard father, Vidhya couldn't help feeling happy for her.

"I don't blame them," Amitab said with a wry smile. "They are meant for each other but I don't want to make *any* guy rope in Ria just because *I* believed in love marriage and if you haven't forgotten, this is America and I'm not poor."

"Sometimes I wish I was back in India," Vidhya sighed. "Everything would have been simple then."

"Everything *is* simple," Amitab Melhera grinned, "and Arman is someone I trust blindly."

"Ha!" Vidhya ran her fingers through his hair and pulled his mouth closer to hers, tantalising him with each breath she took. "What if she hates you for this?"

Amitab Melhera swallowed hard as his gaze rested on her full lips, "I…I'll think of something."

"Like what?"

"Let's just say…," he murmured softly as he slowly traced her pouty lips with the tip of his tongue, "I don't plan to tell her until she finds out."

1

"I never said I wanted to live here Dad and why are we even having this discussion?" Ria wailed softly as she got down from the sleek, silver Mercedes Benz. "I just wanted to visit Tanvi and Pratinav. Why is there the imposition now? You really don't care about how I feel!"

Ria had been through a long flight and with that she had received the news about staying in India for a while. Delhi, at first sight, seemed to be in total chaos. It was peak summer and despite the traffic buzzing, the weather sweltering and her clothes suffocating her insides, she managed to convince herself that it was not so bad. Maybe skinny jeans and a sweatshirt was a good idea on the long air-conditioned flight.

They had reached their old house, the one that Mom always used to talk about. Only Dad had seemed reluctant to come back. Now, after so many years, he suddenly wanted to come back, but the home she was used to was in the crowded city of Buffalo where she loved to visit lake Erie. She had gone to complete her under-graduation in English from the University of Buffalo, hoping to study more, if possible. Her Dad owned an automobile industry where he manufactured cars that were outrageously over-priced. She knew all this because his clientele included mostly celebrities or industrialists who wanted to show off their wealth. So they had enough money to accommodate three generations without lifting a hand around and a woman had no part in his business. Her Mom never worked for anyone. Dad always took care of things and bought them everything. Sometimes she wondered if that's how he saw her – a woman who needed a man to take care of her.

The prospect was horrifying. At the moment, the last thing she wanted was a man in her life.

"Now why should you presume that we don't care for you?" Vidhya gasped.

Ria met her Mom's eyes and said flatly, "I can never adjust here."

"Really Ria, you have become unbearably unreasonable these days," she muttered, as they unloaded their baggage. "Now, you did say you wanted to get out of New York, right?" Vidhya tried to reason with her daughter.

"Getting out of New York doesn't exactly mean relocating, Mom!"

Vidhya remembered that she had said that in passing but now she felt she was being made to go through a lot and it seemed as if life had come to a halt after the convocation ceremony — especially when hearts break, life seems palpable.

Amitab Melhera cringed slightly as they walked towards their old house, which they had retained ever since they had been staying at New York. It had not been his decision to come back but he realised how Vidhya longed to be back to her roots. At last he had to give in only because it had been easier to say, 'yes' rather than 'no'. After all, he couldn't enter into an argument with his pretty little wife. Loving her was a part of giving her what she wanted and he was blessed enough to give her exactly what she wanted.

"It's not so bad," Vidhya consoled Ria. "You have just finished college and at twenty-one, you can pursue your studies here and work..."

"I don't need career counselling, Mama," Ria snapped and walked into the house.

Amitab looked expressionlessly at Vidhya, who looked close to crying. "Now what's wrong?" he asked softly as he put his arms around her.

"She is so..."

"Spoilt?"

"I was going to say *young*!" Vidhya snapped and when Amitab rolled his eyes, she burst out laughing. "Okay yes, she is spoilt but she had been living there like a princess. India would be hard on her."

"Any new place would be hard on her," his words sounded soothing. "Let her learn it the hard way."

"Since when have you become so tough on her?"

"*Mom! Dad!*" they heard Ria shriek from the kitchen. "The refrigerator is empty! I told you that..."

"Why don't you find your room first?"

Ria let out a loud sigh, hoping to fill some air through the humidity. "Alright, but I want a Coke and a burger. I am hungry."

As Ria flew upstairs, Vidhya shook her head helplessly, "How come she managed to finish college?"

"She likes studying," Amitab put in with a proud grin. "And though she is spoilt to her core, she did manage to get a scholarship for four years."

"Yes," Vidhya smiled, "that's there. I think a change of scene would do her good. She has been too busy pinning her nose into those thick books…"

"Good for me. I didn't have to warn her any time against boys and parties."

"Why are you so worried about her all the time?" Vidhya again flew into a temper. "She will learn her way and you have done a good job."

Amitab chuckled. He loved it when her eyes sparkled in anger, "I'm just easing my fears and you know that."

"Do…," Vidhya had a faraway look in her eyes, "do you think we should tell her now?"

* * * * *

"You want me to *what?*"

Arman Gupta didn't think he had heard right. His father surely hadn't lost his ability to think this soon? How could he even suggest something like that…?

"Take the first flight to Delhi and get married to Ria," Jeevan Gupta had said with a smile that looked sickening to Arman. "Did you hear me now?"

"I think you are losing your mind. I'm *not* going to India…I'm *not* going to get married to…whatever her name is. Did you get that?"

"I have already promised Amitab and you didn't protest that time…"

"I didn't have a mind of my own then," he countered, ready to leave.

"Sit down!" his father thundered just as he began to move towards the exit. Stiffening his back, Arman turned and stood by his father's desk, shaking his head in a mocking query, "You want to say something?"

"Yes!" thundered Jeevan Gupta, thinking that he hadn't seen a more obstinate man in his life. Agreed that he was an exact clone of his own adulthood but God, why did he have to be *so* like him? Looking at Arman now, almost twenty-eight, he had never seen a more handsome man. In fact, maybe God had stopped making men like Arman. He was tall and pleasantly gold complexioned with eyes startlingly grey. His eyes were like small beads, making their grey colour look dramatic. A thin frame of glasses adorned his sharp nose, completing the executive look. At that moment he wore a stark white, full-sleeved shirt with a pair of black trousers, making him look cunningly masculine. Half the office staff, a few men included, was crazy about him. Not that Jeevan blamed them.

And the most endearing part was that Arman Gupta was oblivious to all the attention he received. He worked when he was supposed to and played when he wanted to. Unfortunately Jeevan couldn't specify when Arman really played. There were no women in his life that Jeevan could point out and say, *yes* at last he is in love. Arman looked the same when he came back from spending his weekend alone or with a woman. Lucky, Jeevan thought, that Arman had *not* fallen in love. Amitab, being his closest friend, had already agreed to Ria being Arman's future wife. So he had by no means encouraged Arman's feelings towards any women. Now he regretted that decision. Arman took life too seriously, he felt.

"You know that you are engaged?"

Arman pushed his glasses back into place and raised a brow, "You also told me that it would be my choice whether to marry her or not. Dad, I *don't* know her!"

Jeevan nodded, "Yes, you were an impressionable twenty-four-year old. I didn't want to impose anything on you then…"

"So you mean you are imposing on me right now?"

Jeevan bit his tongue to stop himself from laughing out aloud at his son's incredulous expression, "I said I wanted to be fair. That means I want to be fair to Ria too. If you meet her and find you are not attracted to her…," Jeevan tried to find a word, shifting uncomfortably when Arman smiled back.

"You mean physically or visually?"

This time Jeevan did laugh out aloud and it felt good too. "What is important to you?"

Grinning for the first time, Arman gave the most obvious answer, "Physically definitely."

"Then I'm sure you could work up some of that charm on Ria."

"Dad…," Arman began to warn him, "I'm not serious about getting married…"

"Why?" Jeevan snapped, narrowing his eyes. "Are you dating someone?"

Arman tried not to feel offended, "As a matter of fact, Dad...yes I'm dating...," Jeevan tried not to turn pale. "Cristina is not a bad girl...so stop looking at me that way."

"Are you planning to marry her then?"

"No."

At Arman's rough tone, Jeevan knew that he wasn't lying.

"So you are just sleeping with her," Jeevan shrugged. "You can always drop her if you want to. You have to marry your own kind..." When Arman didn't banter back, Jeevan added softly, "And you know, how wonderful it would be to see you married! You are old enough to have children now!"

Arman choked on a laugh, "Oh Dad, you will never change."

"Well, at least tell me when you plan to go to India?"

"Not to marry her."

"Oh yes, you are going to marry her," Jeevan asserted impatiently. "Don't you ever plan to get married?"

"I don't have to get married if that's what you are indicating."

"Haven't you heard the saying in Bible, 'It is not good for the man to be alone and marriage was God's solution to loneliness'?"

"The Bible cannot solve my problems and I'm not lonely."

"Atheist!" shot back Jeevan, smiling uneasily.

Arman straightened and started to walk out of his father's office, "I'll see her and meet her, but don't expect miracles overnight."

"What if you were to at least *like* her?" Jeevan put in helpfully.

Arman turned and winked at his father, "Then I'll sleep with her."

Jeevan thought he would faint right in his chair and his expression must have suggested it because Arman came rushing back into the office, "I was kidding, Dad!"

"Oh…okay," said Jeevan, gulping a mouthful of water and glaring at his son. "She is from a *very* good family and Amitab would kill me if you do something like that."

"Wow, then all your fortune would be mine," Arman grinned gleefully, rubbing his hands dramatically.

"Yeah, right," Jeevan chuckled. "Now get out of my sight and give me the good news when you marry her."

Arman opened his mouth to argue but clasped his lips tightly instead, this time ignoring his father's gesture to him to come back and talk. It was difficult to argue further and impossible not to feel cornered.

* * * * *

"If I didn't know you better Dad, I would have almost believed you," Ria Melhera said with a laugh. "Me? And *engaged*?"

It was her third day in Delhi and surprises just wouldn't seem to stop.

Amitab winced but shook his head, "I'm serious. You are engaged."

Ria stopped laughing abruptly and whirled around to look at her mother, "I hope this is some kind of a joke because if it *is,* I am willing to let go."

"Ria!"

"Well?' she asked impatiently, "right now I'm going to meet Pratinav and Tanvi, so I am not in the mood..."

"I don't want to take this as a life-threatening call, Ria," she heard her father's voice from behind her. "It's just someone I want you to meet...," he left the sentence incomplete on seeing her eyes unwilling to withstand any more arguments. "He is very good looking and very successful in life and as far as I know him, he could charm the birds even."

"Who is *he*?"

"Arman Gupta and he is very good looking," he repeated, hoping that the words impressed her. "In fact, when I met him, he was still sporting his boyish looks...," Amitab said with an indulgent smile.

"Has he seen me?"

"Uh no, but..."

Ria threw her hands up and rolled her eyes, "Do you think anyone good looking and handsome would want to marry me...?"

"Of course," Amitab replied and frowned as if he had been personally insulted. "Why wouldn't he?"

Ria showed the beginnings of a smile to say, "Okay Dad, let's meet him."

She walked away with a smug smile on her face and Vidhya looked worriedly at her husband, "I think she is sure that Arman wouldn't want her."

"Why won't he? Ria is a sensible and intelligent girl. It's been only a week since we came here."

"Of course Ria is sensible and intelligent. I know that too, but you do know that she doesn't consider herself to be pretty."

"What has a face got to do with a heart?"

"Men rely on looks more than brains!" Vidhya informed him with a delicate snap.

"That's rubbish!"

Vidhya raised a brow and muttered, "Yeah, *right.*"

2

Ria thought nothing else could have made her feel any more angrier than what had happened. First her parents got her here all the way from America and then they were trying to impose marriage on her!

Great, just great!

Now she had to wait for that guy Arman Gupta and try to pretend that she was happy with this absurd arrangement. She was far from the kind of girl who could pretend about her emotions that she didn't feel. So being happy with the situation was out of the question. She was seriously not ready for marriage…

"Can you believe it?"

Tanvi Melhera nodded, "He is pretty unpredictable."

"I'm sure he found a guy who is *exactly* like him."

"Then be assured he would be good looking."

"I don't want..."

Tanvi didn't know what to say. She was not a beautiful woman but her face had an appealing softness that made most people smile. She wore her hair in a long straight plait that suited her petite frame. A little older and wiser over the years, she was loved by all, especially by Ria. She had seen Ria when she was a little child and now as a twenty-one-year old, she didn't care much for beauty. Too much like her, though bolder in every sense. In fact all she knew about her niece, Ria was a young woman who would love to be pampered by her man and expect people to do things for her.

"Where's Pratinav?"

"He's in London. Gone for some work; he won't be back for a while."

"And to think that I came here to meet you guys!" Ria muttered to herself. "Stay with us for a while."

"I'll be around and I did come to see you last month in New York. Have you thought of what you plan to do when Arman comes here?"

"I won't marry him," Ria declared as she blew away her hair which fell over her eyes, hindering her vision.

"Why don't you meet him and find out what kind of a person he is?"

Shrugging nonchalantly, Ria rolled her eyes mischievously, "I don't know what kind of a person he would be – good or bad, I'm not marrying him."

"But, why?"

"Shush! I got an idea" Ria winked at her. "I'm in love with someone else. That's what I will tell him! As far as I know, it works all the time."

Tanvi furrowed her brow in confusion – Ria in love with someone?

* * * * *

Arman Gupta never pictured coming back to India, the land of his ancestors. His only link to India was his mother who was raised here, in the northern plains of Punjab. Some day he had hoped to visit the land, perhaps. Somehow he couldn't feel any connection when he noticed the road-sign 'Greater Kailash' at the end of the road, but he was an Indian. He couldn't say he was a pure breed. Too bad he had come with an accent.

A supposed-to-be posh colony of Delhi, he could still find faults. As he passed by the lanes and the overcrowded streets, his eyes noticed the shabby and littered sidewalk, the air pollution and the continuous honking of cars. This was to be expected after he had heard stories from his clients about how much they would have preferred to stay abroad than in Delhi.

He designed cars for a living and he was pretty good at it. Having acquired a degree in both automotive and industrial design, he had joined his father's company. He loved his work and the money that came with it because it provided him all the luxuries that he desired. His only regret was that luxury couldn't provide him the much coveted peace of mind that he longed for.

Right then his mind was on the woman he was supposed to go and get engaged to. Or, was it to get *married*? Just the thought of it was enough to make him see red and he couldn't stop blaming himself for giving in to his father's whims. He didn't want to become a victim of such marital hypocrisy. He was happy with his life abroad, wasn't he? Work was going on exactly the way he wanted and women had never been a problem. In fact, he thought, with a wolfish grin to himself, that he had a personal life which he wouldn't sacrifice for a girl he had never met.

From the way his father had told him about her, she seemed like a young woman who had been brought up on a bed of roses, who loved to sit at home and twiddle her thumbs. And that was what he definitely didn't like; he wanted a wife who would match his calibre – passionate, independent, exciting and sizzling in bed.

Of course, he wouldn't have liked her to have had a good time before getting married to her. He would most probably want a virgin.

He groaned when the cab came to an abrupt halt. He looked out, craning his head through the small window of the taxi. He saw a huge villa where Amitab lived now. It was beautiful yet intimidating. Also, it seemed like many families had lived here; must be ancestral property!

He had met Amitab Melhera four years ago and had been impressed by him. He couldn't deny that he found the man admirable, but doing business with him didn't mean he wanted to marry his daughter. God, he was in a mess and surprisingly enough, he could still recall their conversation.

"I have a daughter," Amitab Melhera had told him and he had pretended interest.

"Oh, what does she do?"

"She's still in school, turned sixteen this May and I'm worried about it."

Arman chuckled, "If she's still in school, why do you have to worry?"

"I'm afraid she will not find a good match here," said Amitab, staring hard at him. "Unless, of course, you..."

"I can't help you out," he immediately responded, dismissing the issue at the mental level. "I hardly know anyone of my age..."

"You could marry her," Amitab had said, enjoying the look of shock on his face.

"I...*could*?"

He still remembered the gleam in Amitab Melhera's eyes, as if he had found some hidden treasure. "Yes, that would be perfect. You could meet her when you are ready, of course. I'll talk to your Dad about this and I am sure he would be ecstatic to hear this."

"Uh...but...," was all he could mutter, forgetting how to say a point-blank 'no'. He had just got into family business and had not even got a complete hang of things when this man, no doubt a lucrative client, was making an impossible offer.

When he thought over it, he felt it was his own fault. He should have been more assertive. Getting out of the cab, he fumbled with the Indian currency that he had been handed at the airport. He knew he was not going to stay here for a long time, so he had exchanged as little cash as possible. It was a good thing that he knew what the rate of conversion was. Paying the cab driver what he asked for, Arman moved towards the villa.

He opened the gate and heard it creak. He stood and viewed the flowers in full bloom and the greens in the front. It did look well maintained and beautiful. He picked up his large bag and adjusted the shoulder strap of his laptop bag on his shoulder.

Then he noticed a girl walk towards him. She wasn't close enough for him to see her face but he could not fail to notice the thick black curls on her head that reached her waist. She had an exquisite pixie-like figure – too short, he decided, but then, short girls were exciting to make love to. In fact, one interesting position was to make love while seated on a chair, and suddenly he couldn't help but visualise her naked on his lap, riding him up and down with intense ardour. He felt himself going hard somewhere down and closed his eyes as best as he could.

He was here to get married for God's sake! No, he wasn't. He wasn't going to get married to anyone.

When he opened his eyes next, he found her standing right in front of him.

Ria Melhera tilted her head and raised a delicate brow, "You know something…?" she said impetuously. "You are trespassing."

"Am I?"

Blinking, Ria found his voice to be thick and different. She had never heard a man talk in that voice here in Delhi; it seemed as if he had an accent. Since she sported one too, she couldn't help but smile.

"You don't live here, do you? Where are you from?"

Her question must have surprised him because he stood staring hard at her, as if assessing her. And the way he studied her was rather unusual. No one looked at her to convey that they found her attractive…

He was tall, very tall, she thought as she tilted her head up to talk. And his spectacles suited him. On peering closer, she was shocked to find herself gazing into sparkling grey eyes. God, he looked so dynamic. And his hair was thick and long. No one could miss the mop of hair which had been combed neatly at the back of his head into a pony tail with an all-black band.

"You are right, I'm not from here..."

"Are you sure you are not trespassing?" she asked again, now curious about the stranger more than ever.

"Actually I'm supposed to be. This is Mr Amitab Melhera's house, right?"

Her eyes shifted from his hair and she said in a distracted voice, "Hmm...yeah, it is. But I don't suppose he is expecting any callers unless you are...," for a moment Ria paused and then her eyes widened in shock. She automatically took a step back and asked, "You...*you* are Arman Gupta?"

He raised a brow and Ria swallowed again. He was *the* sexiest man she had ever had the opportunity to meet. If only she could stop telling this to herself...!

"I'm glad you know me. Am I supposed to remember your name too, sweetheart?"

Sweetheart?

This time it was Ria who looked a little wary, "If I wanted you to remember my name, *sweetheart*...," she mocked, "I would have made sure that you would never forget me."

Arman felt a hot flow of blood singe through his loins. She was arousing him and she was hardly aware of that. The way her sassy mouth worked was playing havoc with his insides.

A closer look revealed it wasn't as striking as he had expected it to be. In fact, she looked like a girl who liked to keep a low profile. Her hair looked naturally curled, yet they were untamed enough to reach her waist. Arman had never seen a girl more pretty, he thought, pausing a full second.

He had never considered any woman pretty. They were either simply sexy or hot for him; but here was a girl who was affecting him, he decided, as much as he hated to admit it.

"Would you mind telling me your name?"

"Oh…you would find out *eventually*," she muttered as she looked at his bags closely. "Are you planning to stay for long?"

"Maybe…," his eyes paused at her lips. "If I were offered an attractive incentive, I might."

"Oh!"

Her lips were devoid of lipstick and were in a normal baby pink shade. He wanted to bite them and drive that chaste look away.

Ria took another step back and gestured with her head towards the entrance, "You can go in."

"In a minute," he whispered. "Can I know your name first?"

She shook her head, "I told you that you will find out."

"So sure?" his voice teased.

Ria felt a burst of heat surge through her face. Couldn't he just leave her alone and go inside? He did not even know who he was talking to and if he found out that she was his would-be fiancée, then? Ha, big joke! She had no intention of marrying him anyways. Maybe she should tell him right away. She opened her mouth to tell him just that when he moved closer and placed his finger right on her lips. Gulping with shock, Ria's eyes flew wildly up at him but his eyes remained focused right on her lips. He seemed so curious about her lips!

She had thought that her lips were the last thing on her face that people would ever notice first; it was always her hair that they did. Today of all the days she had misplaced her band which invariably kept her hair in place. She drew in her breath abruptly and almost choked on it when his finger moved as a caress on her lips. It moved first to her upper lip, tracing the shape as the tip of his thumb moved to the lower one. His caress was softer than a feather's touch. He took her lower lip between his thumb and forefinger and squeezed it lightly. Ria tried unsuccessfully to stop the palpitations of her heart beating at full speed.

"What was *that*?" she asked, surprised to find her voice soft and husky.

Arman stepped back, carefully fisting his palms tightly. There was almost a dangerous look in his eyes as he breathed slowly, blowing air in and out. "You shouldn't have let me do it," he said.

To that Ria had no answer. The feel of his fingers still lingered on her lips, which felt marauded thoroughly.

"I...," Ria narrowed her eyes, wanting to erase the image and feel of those expert hands on her. "You didn't tell me what that was."

He met her eyes and his grey eyes held a definite twinkle as if he couldn't believe he was being asked this question. "It was a...kiss."

Ria felt her temper fly. How dare he? The flirt, the...*the*...

"You must be wanting to go inside," she said pointedly in a tight voice.

"Yes...but..."

"I have to go," Ria muttered and turned her back on him, walking as fast as her feet could carry.

"When will I see you again?" she heard him say loudly and this possibly made her parents inside aware that someone was at the door.

"Soon," was all she could manage to reply.

Arman Gupta sat in front of Amitab Melhera and tried not to feel daunted. Somehow it was impossible to sit quietly and be stared at for long. Just the presence of him oozed power and luxury. On any other occasion, he would have loved to talk to this man but at that moment, it seemed almost embarrassing to voice his thoughts.

"I'm glad you are here...," Amitab Melhera said. Arman Gupta shrugged, "Hmm...it's been long since I was here..."

Frowning, because he was not aware of this, Amitab asked politely, "How long has it been?"

"Twenty-eight years."

"You *are* twenty-eight-years old," asked Amitab.

"That's right."

"So this is your first visit here..."

They both stared at each other for a long moment before bursting out into laughter, hiding their amusement under loud coughs.

Looking at Arman, Amitab Melhera thought complacently that he had chosen the right guy for his daughter, for after all, a good sense of humour was necessary to keep a marriage going.

"About Ria…," Amitab began but stopped when he noticed the younger man's expression go blank all of a sudden. It was a face that people used when they didn't want to show any emotions.

"You did know that you are engaged, right?"

"Yes," said Arman as he couldn't deny that fact. In fact when he had said 'yes' to Mr Melhera's proposal for his daughter, it had been pure instinct. What had made him say 'yes' was indeed a quirk of his mind or was it fate? The thought made him so gloomy and trapped that he wished to get up and leave. Just a few minutes ago he had been attracted to a woman and now he found himself in a situation where he was discussing his forthcoming marriage to Ria. Come to think of it, being engaged hadn't stopped him from having affairs. Though he had kept himself emotionally unattached, he could hardly say the same thing about his body. He hadn't even informed Christina about this absurd engagement.

"Then you should be happy about it," he heard Mr Melhera say quietly.

Oh, so he was expected to feel happy about it? Not in a million years was he ever going to be happy with such an arrangement. Maybe he should just break it all up…but again, something inside him held him back. It was his future father-in-law sitting in front of him rather than a businessman now.

"You do remember that I specifically *wanted* you to marry my daughter?"

"Yes...," Arman held his breath. "But Dad and I discussed it after you left and you didn't let me even meet Ria..."

"She was too young to get involved in such a sort of arrangement and it would have only distracted her from studies."

"I know that...," Arman knew that this discussion was leading them nowhere. After all, what kind of a father would let his sixteen-year old daughter date a twenty-four-year old guy? A bitter regret began to gnaw at his heart...

"You must be thinking I'm a horrible father."

"No...," Arman murmured. "You did the right thing for yourself, but I'm not sure about marrying your daughter, Mr Melhera."

"I beg your pardon?"

Arman tilted his head, "I admire and respect you...I always did, but I can't marry Ria."

"Did I hear my name being called?"

Arman whipped his head around and his eyes widened with shock.

3

"Uh…yes," Amitab said, still frowning at Arman as he raised his cheek absently for her to kiss him. "This is…"

"Arman Gupta," Ria chirped. "Yes I know."

Arman Gupta grimaced with irritation and thought, so she did know that it was *him*. Then why didn't she introduce herself there and then? And here he had been thinking about having an affair with her. Now he realised that it wouldn't be that easy; at the same time it wouldn't be easy to forget her.

This was the woman he was supposed to marry and not have an affair with! He suddenly remembered what his father had told him – good girls don't have affairs.

"We were just talking about you," Amitab murmured, his brow wrinkled thoughtfully at Arman's earlier statement.

"Oh *really?*" Ria moved quickly to sit down beside her father. "I would like to know what you both were discussing about me."

"Now Ria...don't start..."

"No...it is *you* who has started all this," Ria hissed back in a low voice. Staring back at Arman, Ria bit back a sigh. He *was* very good looking, there was no doubt about it, but arrogance was written clearly on his face. The way his eyes moved within his thin frame of glasses...gosh, it was easy to stare at him for hours.

"Do you want to say something Miss Melhera?"

"Do I *have* a say?" she shot back, suppressing a smile that waited to make its appearance.

"I would like you both to meet in a proper way!" Amitab Melhera growled. "And if you want to turn this into a farce, then I'm going to have to ask Arman to leave."

Ria smiled and tilted up her head as if in victory. But Arman was not a raw hand and he knew that if she wanted to play dirty, then so could he.

"No...I think I would like to meet your daughter the...," he hesitated for a second, threw an unfathomable glance at Ria before continuing, "*the* proper way, like you want."

"What about what I want?" Ria snapped and scrambled out from the sofa. "If either of you think that I'm going to surrender submissively to this distorted scheme, then you both have another thing coming!"

"*Ria*!"

Arman somehow liked the way Ria reacted and he could not understand why it was so. Never in his life had he met women who had dared to say what they wanted. So Ria was indeed a surprise to him. He admired her for the way she stood up for herself, but hated to admit that he didn't like the way she was glaring at him, as if it all had been *his* fault.

"I told you before Dad that this is not going to happen...I'm not going to marry anyone..."

"Won't you at least listen to your father?" Arman intervened, leaning back on the sofa and making himself comfortable. "I'm sure you are getting heated up for nothing. We all are adults here. You will have what you want. Now...," he said, motioning towards the sofa, "if you were to just sit down..."

Ria frowned fiercely at him but sat down obediently.

"Why don't you show Arman his room for now?" Amitab Melhera heaved a sigh of relief.

"I don't want to..."

"It's alright Mr Melhera," Arman got up gracefully. "We can discuss this later at dinner."

"Yes, alright."

Ria opened her mouth to protest but realised that all her entreaties would fall on deaf ears for neither of the men was prepared to listen. And where had her mother gone instead of supporting her?

If only...

"Ria, show Arman his room," Amitab told her firmly.

She frowned again, "*What*...now I *have* to..."

She felt Arman's hand curl firmly around her upper arm and grip her tightly. She just stopped herself short from gasping out loud at the warmth of his touch. It felt good to be held like that.

Ria was a loner as far as she knew. No one really bothered to talk to her and make small talk even; all that they ever wanted from her was either her notes, or her projects, or her ideas. She could not fathom what was going on. Her mind and body sizzled at his touch. Outside, when Arman had touched her lips, she had realised what he was capable of doing to her. The one time that she had given in to her desire had not made her feel the way he could. That had been a mistake but she didn't want to make another one.

"Just show me where my room is…I'll go by myself."

"Oh…okay. Follow me," she tried to pull away from him but his hand retained its. She wanted to jerk his hand away but seeing that her father wasn't in the mood for any of her tantrums, she kept her mouth tightly pursed. "I don't want you to touch me. *Ever*!" she hissed.

Arman Gupta raised his brows and moved his hand slowly away from her arm. "Does it bother you that much? My touch?"

"No!" Ria spit out as she moved to leave him.

"What's making you this angry then?" she heard him ask behind her, the calm in his voice disturbing her equilibrium. "I understand you are annoyed at your parents for fixing your marriage when you weren't even sixteen…"

"I'm sure it doesn't bother you much."

"No, you are wrong. It bothers me and I yelled at my father too."

Ria turned and faced Arman with some curiosity, "And?"

"And he told me to go to India and get married."

"Oh!" Ria lost all hope, as she had expected a ray of hope to save her from this predicament.

"But I did tell your Dad that I don't want to marry you," he said. She noticed a naughty gleam in his eyes as he continued, "But that was before I knew who you were."

"What does that mean? I would have refused even if I had met you," Ria snapped, her heart beating at an unhealthy rhythm. "Now, don't say you want to marry me?"

Arman didn't think he wanted to refuse now. This Ria Melhera was totally different from the women he had known or dated and felt that getting to know her might actually prove to be fun. She was full of spirit and raw sexuality waiting to be explored, though her dislike of him did bother him much. Perhaps that could be the reason why he didn't want to give in to his father's wishes either. She was not bad to look at either – a little plump around the edges but possibly it would feel great to hold her. And she had gorgeous lips!

"Why do you think I'm going to refuse now?"

"Because *I* don't want to marry you."

Arman couldn't help but smile, "I can't miss the opportunity of being called your husband."

Narrowing her eyes, Ria tilted her head to one side and said menacingly, "Will you or will you not refuse?"

"You can refuse too."

"What do you think I was doing out *there*? Cracking a joke?"

Arman looked lazily at her and shook his head, "No, you seemed too desperate and that wouldn't work, you know. Your father is just too clever for you. Remember the saying, 'empty vessels make the most noise'."

"What? Do you mean that I didn't mean what I said out there?" she asked, her hands on her hips and her eyes glaring at him.

"Maybe you meant it," he sighed and took his glasses off,

closing his eyes and pinching the bridge of his noise. "I'm *damn* tired."

"Oh!" Ria had not thought that she too was tired because after all she had come to Delhi only a week ago and the fourteen-hour-long flight had almost killed her. She should have understood that Arman would be more than just tired because the long flight was no less than a third degree torture for someone who was not used to travelling this far.

"You should rest then."

He paused for a second and opened his eyes. Ria swallowed hard, thinking that his eyes looked better without glasses. In fact, he looked different when he didn't wear glasses. She began to wonder what his hair would look like if left unbound!

Biting her lips hard to stop herself from giving vent to her thoughts, she turned to go out. All that staring had cost her peace of mind.

It hadn't gone unnoticed either. "Do you like my eyes?"

Ria gasped and gave him an incredulous look, "You have the nerve…!" Arman started laughing and she burst out, "I have seen eyes more beautiful than yours!"

"Oh, really?"

"*Look* Mr Gupta…"

"Yes Miss Melhera?"

She noticed how much he was enjoying the process of unnerving her. His smile was almost polite and she needed no sympathy from him.

"Whose eyes are more beautiful than mine?" he asked blandly.

"Someone…," Ria muttered because she couldn't exactly

remember any name. Her mind was still relishing the sight of his eyes for they were truly resplendent.

"A man's?"

Ria felt it was more than a polite query and she threw at him, "Yeah."

"Oh? A boyfriend?"

"You wouldn't want to know that," she returned sweetly.

"Right."

Ria turned away, losing interest in the topic or rather she didn't know what to say to that. If he wanted to know about her personal life, then he could just go to hell. As if she was in any mood to tell anyone what or whom she liked!

"I have a distinct feeling that you don't want to tell me anything."

"After the way you just behaved outside my house, think again, buster!"

The words were out before she could stop and she felt Arman move behind her and place a hand on her shoulder, "You want me to apologise for that?"

"I don't think you are sorry enough Mr Gupta and I think I asked you not to touch me."

"Now you are being childish."

"I have a right to say anything childish when it comes to anyone touching me."

"*God*…you have a sharp tongue."

"Not God, Mr Gupta…me. I have a sharp tongue."

"You are tempting me into experiencing that tongue of yours."

"And I'm tempted to leave you alone right now."

Arman saw her walk away with her head held high. He knew she was just short of turning and hitting him squarely on his face but her good sense prevailed and that is when she left him alone. Maybe she was just agitated at the entire situation.

But he didn't feel any agitation himself. In fact just the thought of how he would have loved to roll his tongue around hers made him want to pull her back into his room. But that wouldn't do…

Being experienced should have taught him that taking any risk was not one of his qualities, *especially* when it came to his personal life. He would not have liked to see his affair turn dirty before it started, and starting or ending an affair with Ria would only lead him either out of business or out of his own moral ethics. God, he was indeed in a mess, but he couldn't help feeling attracted to her.

Ria thought they had nothing more to say to each other but as she passed across his door, she noticed Arman open it. She paused, even though she didn't know why!

"Oh…good you are here."

"Am I supposed to be happy too?" Ria stood still, seeing him grin.

"I can't seem to find the switch for hot water."

"Oh…"

Ria tried not to peek in, "I don't think it's that difficult to find…"

"I have been waiting for someone to pass by my door, Ria and…," his teeth chattered suddenly, "just tell me…?"

"Oh, *alright*!" Ria said, entering inside. "Move aside…"

She had expected Arman to at least be decent when she

entered but all she saw him do was to pick a towel and wrap it around his hips causally. She could not fathom why he felt cold in an air-conditioned room when she felt perfectly fine. Thank God, she had enough sense to turn around when she had the chance or else…

"Well?" she heard the impatience in his voice. "I'm freezing and this room's air-conditioner is still on."

"Then you should have worn something!"

She felt him hesitate behind her, "I'm sorry…I didn't realise…"

Now he was apologising…!

She began to visualise a picture of him with his tall frame without clothes...Already she found him appealing with clothes and all. Now she told herself that she was behaving like a mental patient briefly maybe, but she knew that Arman Gupta was not a desk jockey.

She looked down at herself and felt the desire to work out. Only when she felt strange emotions engulf her did she realise how unattractive she must look to Arman. He seemed to work out for those abs were enough proof of it. How would it be to touch…?

She felt a chill run down her spine and she turned abruptly, "The switch is on the right side…beside the geyser."

"You should take a solar heater."

"Do you think this is the right time to worry about global warming?" he chuckled and stopped when she glared at him.

"We haven't been here for years…Dad was thinking of renovating the entire house."

The switch was completely beyond her reach, but determined to do something as she was there, she raised herself on her toes, "If you could just reach *it*..."

"Here."

She was just half away through it when she felt a strong pair of hands lift her above the floor. She squeaked with fear at first before shouting out angrily, "What are you *doing*?"

"Helping you. What else do you think I...*oh no*..."

"W...what?"

"My towel..."

"What happened to your towel?"

Here she was in the air while the stupid man was worried about his stupid towel.

"It just came off."

"Oh!" Great, now he was truly naked.

Ria swallowed hard, thinking that if she were to start kicking her legs like a desperate damsel in distress, he would not be able to handle her. Most probably they would stumble on each other and end up lying over each other. Then she knew that wouldn't be able resist...

"Now switch it on."

"Uh...yeah," she pulled the switch up and felt goosebumps creep up and make her shiver. "Will you please lower me down?" she said gruffly.

"Okay, but don't turn around," he warned her and she didn't think he was joking about it.

"Alright, but let me down first!"

"Chill!"

"You *chill* and..."

"You are very short, Ria," he said and she could hear the amusement in his voice.

"Then you should find yourself a taller girl…one who could match yours!" Ria said, reprimanding him with a glare. However, his words about his towel kept ringing in her ears.

"I want you to put me *down*…"

Suddenly she was on her feet and the imprint of his fingers lingered for long on her waist. She wanted to turn desperately and shriek, but curbed her desire.

"I have you safe. Don't think too much about it."

"*How*…," Ria did the mistake of turning and saw that he was stark naked.

She saw him close his eyes as if in pain, "I told you not to turn…*and* I wasn't being prude about it."

Then she understood why he had warned her not to do so. Looking up from his toe to his face, she realised he was capable of making any female fall on her knees and worship him. He was six feet and no matter where she looked, she could see only flesh and muscle, especially his muscles which were noticeable. Her breath caught in her throat and she tried to breathe. There was plenty of hair sprinkled everywhere and he looked so masculine that she wanted to feel if they were rough or soft. Moisture still clung to his body while his hair was coiled tightly behind his head. Vaguely she felt that she could no longer stand still on her feet and she felt an overpowering urge to sit down.

"Ria, please leave."

Her eyes met his gravely, "I know I should leave…," she tried to tear her eyes away from his and started to walk out.

Arman thought he was going to faint and not because he

felt cold; it was because Ria had stared at him while he had felt like sinking through the floor. Had it been anyone else other than Ria, he wouldn't have waited for her to look at him the way she had. He would just have picked her up and taken her to bed. But then any other woman wouldn't have made him feel that way either. However, he couldn't let her know how she had the power to affect him. He couldn't give that kind of power to her or to *any* woman and in any case, he had promised himself that he was not going to bed her. Too much was on stake.

4

Arman came down, only too willingly this time. He hoped to see Ria. He was calmer and thoughts about her clung to his mind like glue. Somehow her anger delighted him and made him want to go along with Amitab's insane idea of getting married. He found them both in the sitting room. Ria sat glumly, while Amitab had a satisfied expression on his face. This was one stubborn father!

"Hello all."

Ria didn't even look at him but Amitab began by suggesting, "Why don't you two go out?"

"Why?" Ria snapped.

"Try asking 'where'?" Arman intervened. "He's sending you out anyway."

Ria looked at her father with determined eyes, "I'm *not* going."

"You should go. How else would you come to know him?"

She dug her heels firmly in the ground, "I know him well enough to reject him."

Amitab chuckled embarrassedly, "She is just kidding."

Arman didn't think she was and his eyes glinted behind his glasses, "I'm not forcing you to marry me."

"Then prove it. Tell him that you don't want me."

He raised a brow and his eyes assessed her body with an insolence that infuriated her, "I cannot lie."

"Well, can't you go on a date for my sake?" Amitab asked, looking downcast and using the only weapon he thought could work for the moment.

Somehow her father sending her on a date wasn't something that Ria hankered for. She wanted to yell at both the men for trying to dominate her life. On second thoughts, she couldn't disappoint her father either and it would be a good opportunity to tell Arman outright that she was not interested in him. No matter how annoying this man could be, he didn't irritate her to the extent of making her shun him.

Condescending to Amitab's suggestion, she agreed reluctantly, "Oh, alright. I guess there is no harm," though looked utterly miserable when saying it. For a moment even Arman looked uncertain.

"Go now then."

"*Now*?" Ria echoed blankly.

"I'll give you time to change," Arman offered generously, receiving an exasperated look from Ria.

"I'm wearing this; like it or not!"

Arman eyes danced devilishly as he eyed her outfit. She didn't look fit to be out of the house but the jeans and the

T-shirt she wore could have been worse. She looked small, sweet and a handful.

"You have nothing to lose," said Ria, regarding him silently.

Shrugging, Arman gave in, "Let's go then."

Amitab waved at them indulgently as they walked out of the house, "Take the car!"

As soon as they were out of hearing range, they felt irrationally indecisive. Arman, with both his hands in his pockets, looked at Ria, waiting for an outburst.

"I want to walk," Ria couldn't help adding, "and where are you taking me?"

"Since you make the decisions for yourself, don't ask me this question," Arman said, walking determinedly. In fact he needed the air to cool his brain and other parts of his body. He had been under a lot of stress, thinking about this little nymph and this was their first outing! Why he was attracted to her when she clearly didn't want him troubled his mind. She wondered how else she could have made her intentions clearer!

As they crossed the main gate of her house, he observed that the roads were empty of the usual traffic, except for a bike or two. He didn't know what he could conclude about Delhi but then, it didn't disgust him either. Maybe he needed to explore the city more the next day.

"You should at least know where we are going. How would we come back?" Ria asked him worriedly as minutes passed away and they continued to walk silently.

"How would I know? I was not born in India..."

"As if I know! I left India when I was three, as must have

been conveyed by my parents," she slumped her shoulders, her hair swinging gently with the swing of her arms. Arman was having a hard time not noticing anything about her.

"What if I tell you my real Dad had left us?" Ria's voice came from far off. "And I'm telling you this because I'm hoping this piece of information puts you off..."

"That you are not actually a rich man's daughter?" he asked infuriatingly. "I have enough money of my own. In any case, where is your biological father?"

She shrugged uncertainly, "I haven't tried to probe much but it seems like I never knew him."

"I see," he said, staring at her. Somehow her story struck a sore note in him and he narrowed his eyes. Ria noticed that odd look on his face, "*What*?"

"I lost my mother when I was sixteen. I just remember my Dad crying...," his voice trailed off as his pace increased.

Trying to walk with him was not easy now. So far she had not thought of Arman as a man with feelings and emotions. She considered him a pain in the neck and nothing more but noticing the emotions in his voice, she wanted to empathise. His good looks could easily make her fall for him, but she was not looking for looks in a man. Appearances didn't make for a lasting marriage. Her gaze fell helplessly on his face before coming to rest on his lips. They were thick and plump...

"Why didn't he remarry?" she asked, just to change the train of her thoughts.

"He said he loved her too much," prompt came the answer.

"No other women?"

"I never saw him with someone. Somehow I resented what he was doing with his life," Arman growled. "He drowned himself full heartedly in his company…"

"I would like to meet him."

Arman gave a harsh sigh, "My Dad's very cheerful most of the times. You won't find in him a man still grieving for his wife."

Ria grinned, "You love him."

They had walked far enough now and Arman regretted opening up to her. After all, he didn't know her well enough to talk to her that way. Moreover she didn't like him. What was it about her that made him pour his heart out?

"But you have women in your life."

"I'm not a saint!" he snapped and Ria froze at the tone of his voice.

"Neither am I!" she said, looking angry now as she began to walk briskly as if to prevent any further cross-examination.

"You had boyfriends?" he asked in a voice laced with disbelief and sarcasm.

Ria tried to match his pace, failing most of the times. "You already asked me this question and I *did have* a boyfriend, if you really want to know."

Suddenly Arman stopped walking and bumped into her, "Ria, we are getting to know each other."

She looked dubious and her words faltered, "I…I guess."

"You don't want to marry me, right?" They were facing each other now and he sounded hurt for a moment.

"Of course not."

"Then let's stop asking questions."

They turned back and took the same road home. It was

not very difficult to find their way back. Amitab's villa could be seen from far away and though the detailing of the building could make a stranger stop and admire, both of them seemed oblivious to such artifice. Arman owned a decent enough apartment back home. He was not too keen on owning houses, but surprisingly he wasn't missing his lonely apartment either. Ria walked in front of him and he couldn't help staring at her back. She walked swiftly and her hair bounced with each movement. She possessed beautiful and long hair, worth touching at least once. What a sad thing that she kept her hair in a no-nonsense style that suited her lifestyle. She didn't look like she wanted to entice him with anything.

Maybe he shouldn't have told her about his mother. He didn't exactly like remembering those vague, despondent memories and he was scared to love the way his father had. Under his cheerful veneer, he had noticed a lonely man.

"Arman," Ria turned and her eyes were shaded in darkness.

"Yes?" he stood far away from her, waiting for her to join him.

"Would you cry if your wife dies?"

He lost his breath for a second but maintaining his equilibrium, he answered honestly, "Ria, if I loved her, I would die if she died."

* * * * *

"Do you mind telling me what you really want?" Vidhya Melhera asked her daughter at the dinner-table.

"I want to be left alone," Ria answered back.

"I'm sorry you had to learn about your engagement this way Ria, but you are not giving Arman a chance…"

"Mom!" Ria lifted her spoon and said, pointing in the direction of Arman's room, "If you think I'm going to give that man a chance, then forget it."

"What's wrong with him?"

"He…his…," Ria slammed her spoon back on her plate. "Well for one, his hair is longer than mine."

Vidhya eyes widened, "Not longer than yours surely?"

"Uh no…but I don't like long hair on guys. I think only gay…"

"You *mean,* surely Arman is not gay, Ria!"

"Mom!" Ria groaned and pushed her plate away. "I don't need to have a reason not to marry him?"

"Can I join in?"

"What were you doing back there?"

Arman Gupta walked towards her with a grim expression on his face. "Let me guess what you would be thinking now. I was eavesdropping? Right?"

"Right!" Ria spat out, "and I don't care if you heard it all!"

"I know you don't care," he shot back with a hard glint in his eyes.

Ria turned away from him and met her mother's serious gaze. Come to think of it, she didn't care what her mother thought. At that moment, she didn't know what to think. Seeing him naked should have made her feel disgusted but all she could think was how beautiful this man was. If only he had kept his clothes on…!

And then their conversation had been too personal for her to forget it. Arman was emerging more like a human being. Not the monster she was hoping he would be. The decision to reject him was getting difficult.

"Ria...," Vidhya said, gritting her teeth. "He is a guest and your fiancé. This is no way to talk to..."

"*Please* Mom!" Ria stood up and glared at Arman. "I think you should tell my Mom what I think about you."

"I think I don't need to tell her. You are doing a very good job of telling her all."

"What?"

"Will you cool down Ria?" Vidhya pleaded softly. "Don't be rude."

Abruptly Ria stopped talking. Early in the morning, Arman looked freshly shaved and had dressed formally. He looked better than any famous movie star. In fact, she wondered if he had done any modelling or was offered any assignment.

"Now you are staring," Arman's amused voice broke into her thoughts.

"You are just too handsome!" she spat and he winced when he heard the words.

"So?" Vidhya's incredulous voice broke in. "Isn't that a good enough reason for marrying?"

"Good thing for whom?" Ria pointed a finger at her face. "Look at me and look at him...if we are together there will be a disaster."

"I beg your pardon?"

Ria wished Arman stopped butting in, but just to clear the scores, she continued, "You are too tall, too good looking, too rich…and I'm short, just okay to look at and I don't have anything in my bank account. And I'm overweight for my own good. I hate fad diets and I can't walk for more than a mile. Does that answer your question?"

Arman sat quietly, stinging inside because the words 'tall', 'good looking' and 'rich' didn't sound like compliments from her. "I never had a problem with your weight. If you have a problem, then you should do something about it."

"I don't have a problem," Ria said defensively.

"I never asked you any question about how we complement each other, Ria."

"Exactly, you didn't even care to ask me that question. See?" her eyes turned towards her mother. "I have got the reason for not marrying him. This man doesn't care."

"Ria…," Vidhya groaned as if in pain. "Stop, will you?"

"*Why*?"

Arman suddenly burst into peals of laughter and both of them turned to look at him with incredulous frowns. Arman knew that it was no time to laugh but the fact was that she was insulting him right on his face and for the world of him, he didn't know why he was not taking offence. Why didn't he just answer her back or just tell her to shut her trap? Maybe he would…when things would get too far, but right then, he seemed to be enjoying the verbal exchange.

A really good break from the everyday rat race…

"At the end of the day, looks do not matter in a marriage, Ria," Vidhya said quietly. "Your Dad is a very handsome man too but he will grow older and then there would be wrinkles on his face, but I will be still younger to him, looking quite different. Do you think that because of that, I would leave him? Simply because I would look better than him?"

Ria blinked her eyes in confusion, "You love him. Even the dead can't make you leave him."

"Exactly."

"But…I…we don't love each other, Mom," Ria said, getting up to leave.

Arman suddenly didn't find it funny any longer and blurted out, "I didn't know that it mattered so much to you."

"I have had enough of this talk."

"Why do you keep on standing and sitting?" Arman enquired softly.

"What…*oh*…," Ria sat back on the chair and then closed her eyes tightly, shaking her head. "I'm going mad."

Fascinated, Arman watched her curls bounce against her cheeks. They looked heated enough to curl around one of his fingers and he had an overpowering urge to weave his fingers through those curls surrounding her face. Her cheeks must be soft and he found the cheekbones prominent. No super model in the world could replace those apple-coloured cheeks of hers. How he would have enjoyed taking a bite on each of them…!

Vidhya Melhera was watching Arman closely, more than watching her own daughter. The look in his was far from any irritation and she was surprised why he *wasn't*. As far as she knew, Ria was definitely irritating the hell out of her! Ria was acting blind to what she had in hand.

It was on the tip of Arman's tongue to say that she

had the most beautiful hair but his eyes suddenly caught Mrs Melhera's. The curious look in her eyes seemed to be asking why he was not trying to get out of the situation.

And she was right. There wasn't a single part of him that wanted to be away from Ria at that moment.

* * * * *

"I'm stuck!"

"With that gorgeous man? Hmm...," Tanvi said, trying desperately not to giggle. "Yes. Dad is the most infuriating person!"

Ria glared at her cousin alias sister-in-law before saying, "I didn't ask for that comment. I just want someone to hear me out."

"I think you did say enough last night."

Arman must have laughed his head off, thought Ria about him.

"You wanted him to get angry?"

"Hmm...I wouldn't have minded."

At least then she wouldn't have to find herself being drawn to his contagious laughter. What was more, his laughter sounded good to the ears. Unfortunately so!

"I don't understand why you don't want to marry him Ria? After all, he has everything that a girl would want."

Ria stared at Tanvi, words bubbling at the tip of her tongue. But she checked herself and drawing herself straight, said defensively, "I just didn't like this high-handedness of Dad."

"Then you should tell him."

"I think he doesn't care. After all, I'm not his daughter

and he thinks I will be happy with his decision." The words were out before she could stop herself and she saw a slow, horrified expression on Tanvi's face, even when she wasn't looking at her. Curiously, Ria turned and found Arman standing at the door just behind her and there was a heavy frown on his face.

"Uh…Arman…hi! Come in," said Tanvi, standing up out of respect. "We were just talking about you."

"Actually," Ria heard a definite edge in his voice, "I want to know why Ria said that."

"What did I say?"

Arman's eyes swung from Tanvi to Ria and they softened indiscriminately, "You know what I heard. You think everyone is against you."

"You heard right," Ria said with a swift nod. "But since it's none of your business, you can butt out."

"Ria…!"

Arman was frowning again and was tempted enough to pick her up, turn her on his knee and give her a sound spanking. The idea was certainly very appealing.

"What she means is that…," Tanvi put in quickly, "Vidhya is my cousin and she married my father-in-law. Then later Dad adopted Ria."

"He already knows that," Ria muttered and got up to leave.

Arman was swift enough as his hand shot out to grasp her by the arm, "Wait."

She raised her eyes and stared at him unblinkingly for a long second. The pressure of his hand increased as if unsure of her obeying his command. She didn't want to. She wanted to jerk his hands away and lick her wounds alone.

"I'll bring something to eat for both of you," Tanvi said wisely and left them alone.

Arman felt as if he was engulfed in dark clouds. Ria did look as if she didn't wanted to talk about it.

"Does it bother you?"

His question was direct and she didn't pretend to misinterpret. "Sometimes, but I do love Dad. He just doesn't listen to me."

"Maybe if our engagement bothers you so much, then you should tell your Dad. *Calmly* but," he added in the end.

"You *tell* him."

"I did tell him, remember? In clear words."

"Then?"

"I think he mostly ignored what I said," Arman said, hiding a smirk and knowing well that a smile was the last thing that Ria wanted him to do.

"*Fine*!" Ria tried to wriggle out of his hold but he held on. "Let me go. I think I told you once earlier not to touch me."

"How do you expect to live with me when we get married?" Arman drawled lazily. "I'm going to touch you all the time then."

Ria's head whipped up and a slow blush began to creep up her cheeks. She was not comfortable with this kind of talk. He looked at her as if he wanted her…

"I don't think you want me to, right?" Arman put in helpfully when he saw how flustered she looked.

"Yes!"

Arman suddenly let her go and she found the act disconcerting. Did he have to be so insensitive about it?

"I have a girlfriend," Arman said suddenly.

Her eyes widened and she frowned. Her heart yelled out the words, '*You are engaged to me and you have a girlfriend!*'

"I think she can help us out."

"How…*how* can your girlfriend help us?"

Arman ignored the bewilderment in Ria's eyes and voice. He wondered what made him mention Christina.

"She's in India at the moment. On work basis…"

"You've met her?"

Arman shrugged, "I spoke to her over the phone. Since neither of us are really interested in getting married, I…"

"You *what*?" Ria didn't realise that her voice had risen to a high pitch.

Arman dug his hands into his pockets and without meeting her eyes, said, "I'll bring her here."

"*What*?"

"You can tell your father what a rake I am and then he will end it all."

Ria stared at him incredulously for several seconds, wondering what it would be like to slap him on his face at least once…for even saying that.

"Didn't like the idea?"

"Don't make me hate you," Ria gnashed each word explicitly.

Surprised, Arman thought what she would say if he told her that he had already slept with Christina. "You like me then?"

"Oh…! Do what you want; I just want to get rid of you!" Ria stormed out of the room, her eyes amazedly misty.

5

Tanvi slipped into the room quietly and saw Arman standing by the window, staring intently at something. Placing the cups of coffee on the table, she moved towards him. Well into her late thirties now, she knew what hardships of life were and how difficult the course of finding true love was. The concept of an arranged marriage and landing here together must have given their brains some mental workout.

"Coffee?" she prompted.

He turned slightly and nodded, "Ria still around?"

"No. I haven't seen her outside anywhere. What did you tell her now?"

Frowning, Arman rubbed his forehead, "She is very sensitive. She has been living in New York for so many years, yet she behaves like a typical Indian girl."

"Ah…I see," Tanvi's eyes crinkled at the sides as she pursed her lips thoughtfully. "Did you try to…?"

"No it's not what you think," he put in immediately. "It's just that she seems very reluctant to even continue with our alliance and I always see her angry and frustrated. I suggested that I could bring in my girlfriend…"

"You have a *girlfriend*?"

"I'm twenty-eight," he replied tightly, "and I didn't quite remember that I was engaged."

"And Dad says that you are *the* best guy he could find for his daughter."

He narrowed his eyes, "No wonder you both are cousins."

"Well…," Tanvi handed him his cup of coffee and turned around to leave. "Ria is not keen on this marriage idea, as you may know. I think Dad is being just stubborn about it. You could go on with your plan…with that girlfriend of yours."

Arman opened his mouth to agree when she dropped a bombshell, "And also because Ria is in love with someone else."

* * * * *

When Ria opened the door, she was surprised to find a foreigner standing in front of her. She had a distinct feeling that this woman was not a stranger to someone living in her house, so she let the stranger in.

"I'm Christina," the stranger informed her and Ria, who had no interest in introductions, just inclined her head, acknowledging her.

"You are a friend of Arman?"

Obviously.

"Uh...yes," she said, flipping her parlour-treated, straight, golden hair behind her shoulders and Ria wanted to chop them off right then and there.

It wasn't that Christina was a beautiful woman that bothered Ria, but the fact that she was Arman's girlfriend made her hate her at sight. That long blond hair, that perfect figure and pearly white skin could be any dark-skinned woman's envy.

"Is he home?"

"Yes..."

"*Chris*!" their heads whipped towards Arman's voice. As far as Ria was concerned, he looked good enough to eat.

Why the hell did she have to think about him in those terms? He was *not* good enough to eat – how was she to convince herself? Why couldn't she find the black turtle-necked shirt old-fashioned instead of noticing how it clung to his well-muscled chest? Why couldn't she find those jeans faded instead of sexy?

Exercising immense self-control, she tried not to look at Arman's tight calf muscles and she turned a wan, sarcastic smile at him, "Seems like your girlfriend knew where you lived."

"She would," he said tightly. "I called her here."

"You did *what*?"

Ignoring her for once, Arman went and met Christina's eyes squarely, "She is my fiancée."

Ria wished she could have disappeared that very moment. The way Christina appraised her made her want to hit Arman right on his head. Why in the hell did he have to tell her *that*?

"Oh, then what am I doing here? Is she is not good enough for you?"

Raising a brow, Arman said something under his breath, "I didn't find out, Christina and I would never find out. You have to do me a favour."

"Oh..."

Seemed as though 'oh' had become her favourite word of late, Ria thought, glaring at the newcomers and hating the fact that they were on more intimate terms than she had assumed earlier.

Christina moved closer and Ria took a step back instinctively. Christina tipped her head to a side as though unhappy to see what didn't make her happy.

"She is not what you would exactly call thin."

"I didn't call you here to give her one of your aerobic classes," Arman said, folding his arms across his chest. "We have decided not to marry after all and her father is forcing us to..."

"You are not a little kid, you know," Christina said, walking towards Arman. She stretched out a hand and playfully caressed his cheek, "No one can force you into anything."

His eyes crinkled at the sides and Ria fumed inside because she knew he was smirking. This woman could make him smile like that while she...?

"You know me too well Chris...but too much is at stake right now."

"Like?" Ria snapped, her eyes spewing fire.

Arman looked at her uninterestedly, "Like you don't want to get married."

"Of course, I want to marry!" she contradicted. "Just not you in particular though."

"And the reason could be?" Arman narrowed his eyes.

"I don't like you."

"Fine! I don't like you either," he said, turning back to the other woman who was smiling almost maliciously. "And there is nothing better than to get rid of you."

"*Oh*...since when have you become so cruel Arman?" Christina laughed, embarrassed to watch them argue.

Arman met Ria's eyes and paused for a second, "Does it matter?"

"Not to me!" Christina said, looking as if she wanted to rub both her hands together. "What do you want me to do?"

"You could sleep with him," Ria suggested.

Chris looked at Ria with a hard stare, "I have already done. Is that all?"

Ria didn't know how to react to that. Maybe she knew in her heart of hearts that Arman must have been intimately involved with someone but getting the fact thrown right into her face made her want to scratch their eyes out.

And Arman would be the first one.

"Well, I'm sure Arman would appreciate..."

"Enough!" Arman said, no longer look angry. In fact he looked furious. "You can pitch in for the night, Christina."

Ria bit her cheek's inside, wanting to yell at him for making her face all this, when Chris turned towards her, "Will you take my bags inside?" Christina had thrown the words carelessly at Ria.

"Me?" she no longer looked like she wanted to run away

from the scene. "Just why am I supposed to take your bags inside?"

"Chris…," Arman began.

"Do you mind telling her *who* I am Arman?" Ria taunted with an angry sparkle in her eyes.

"No…," said Arman, wishing he could make himself invisible. "Chris she is *my*…," he stopped himself just in time, "Mr Melhera's daughter."

"*Oh*!" Ria had thought that Arman was going to say something else. "She is Amitab Melhera's *daughter*? And you don't want to marry her?"

"Chris, we can talk about this later," and he dragged her away from a livid Ria.

This time Christina looked dumbstruck as she walked away. Ria, confused for a second, looked at Arman as if seeking an explanation.

Arman came back and found Ria eyeing him with distaste. "Your father is counted among the rich and the famous, Ria," Arman explained as if that answered it all.

"So?"

"So it would have been a big event if we would have married…"

"And that's all?"

Arman hesitated for a second and then nodded subtly, "What else could be there?"

"I don't like her," Ria stated, letting go of the conversation for the time being.

"You don't like anyone, Ria. Tell me something new."

Her eyes flashed, "Something new Mr Gupta is that I'm not letting you sleep with her under my roof. You both could go and have a gala time somewhere else."

"I'm your guest."

"You are my supposed fiancé, Arman," came her answer. "I haven't opened a harem."

"This is one way you could be free of me."

"I..." don't want to be...but she swallowed the words immediately. "You are *sleeping* with her?"

Arman looked taken aback. Of all the things, he didn't expect her to say that, so he replied, "I didn't know it mattered..."

"No it doesn't matter but...," Ria frowned trying to think of something, "but you can't dishonour my Dad this way."

"Your *father*...," Arman enunciated disgustedly, "is forcing you to get married. You could marry the man you love and..."

"Man I love?" colour started draining from Ria's face and her face paled abruptly, "*How*...?"

"It doesn't matter how I came to know," Arman cut in. "I haven't had much experience with love but it must mean something to you to keep on opposing this entire situation between us."

Ria's eyes widened, "Haven't had much experience with love?" she pursued her lips tightly. "Why are you so bothered about whom I love? It's not essential that I should marry every man I love."

"You...don't want to marry him?"

"Isn't it obvious? I would have been yelling his name on the top of my voice if I had really wanted to marry him."

"Then why...?"

"He is already married and that's all I have to say." She turned away as thousands of questions came churning in Arman's mind. He however thought silence was the better part of valour.

"Why didn't you tell me about…?"

"I still don't want you to sleep with her," Ria turned, changing the topic.

Arman smiled abruptly, "I'll break the engagement formally. Will that make you happy?"

"And…?"

"Take Chris out of this house?"

Ria just looked at him and answered finally with a despairing sigh, "Well, just take her out of this house. *That* will make me happy."

* * * * *

Christina Baker shook her head bemusedly, "You are letting her go because she is in love with someone else? Since when have rich people bothered about love?"

"Don't be crude Chris," said Arman, closing the door behind him. "Ria is just a kid and she must have some fancy ideas about love…"

"So?"

Arman eyed his girlfriend of three months for a second. Chris recognised that look and began walking towards him, "What are you so pissed off about?"

"Nothing, I want you to leave."

Laughing, Chris shook her head, "I just booked out of that hotel for you. I thought we were spending the weekend together. I won't get the booking again for the next two days."

Arman shook his head a little bemusedly. What was he doing talking to her? He could easily just take her to bed and Ria wouldn't even know. But the fact that he no longer found Chris attractive could be the reason for his stern look. It wasn't right somehow, he concluded grimly.

"Ria doesn't want you to stay here."

"So? I know that already. She is jealous, that's all."

His head snapped at those words, "I have hardly had the chance to know her Chris and I don't have time for this nonsense. She couldn't be jealous of you."

Shrugging her shoulders delicately, Chris walked and closed the door behind him, "Who wants to discuss her?" Moving back, she pressed her body intimately against his. "Let's talk about us," she whispered into his ear, tugging his earlobe with relish.

Arman stiffened for a second and then let himself go with the flow. After all, Chris was his girlfriend. He could indulge himself with her, couldn't he? He tried hard to concentrate on the smell of her hair, the softness of her, but all he felt was disinterest. He just wanted to leave.

"Come on…what's wrong? Kiss me Arman."

"Chris…," he put his hand on both her shoulders and pushed her away. "I'm sorry. You have to leave. I didn't bring you here for this. It was just a big mistake. I can't insult Ria and her parents in this way. I'll get you into a hotel, don't worry."

Frowning fiercely, Chris rolled her eyes in a mocking manner, "Since when did you care about these people? You hardly know them."

"Chris…"

The sudden knock on the door stopped Arman from saying more. He paused for a second before turning to open the door. Ria stood there with literally smoke rising out of her ears.

"I called a cab for her," Ria told him sternly.

He opened his mouth to answer or rather snap at her when Chris drew near Arman and put her arms around his waist fondly, "Oh…Ria, you shouldn't have. I'm not leaving right now."

Turning her attention towards Arman, Ria frowned, "She isn't?"

"I was talking to her about that when…"

"I see." The way Ria was seeing, she didn't think that talking was something that Arman was doing behind closed doors. And she didn't exactly like seeing Chris getting chummy with her fiancée. She halted her thoughts abruptly…

Her *fiancée*? God…she was losing it! She wasn't supposed to feel anything. This was a man she hardly knew. In fact she had met him only a week ago, but did he have to stand so close to this woman?

"Ria…I'm telling you something," Arman said with an exasperated sigh.

"Uh…what?"

He narrowed his eyes as he felt the negative vibes coming from Ria. Why does this woman have to treat him like that? Why couldn't she simply accept that they had to get married?

Damn…! What was he thinking? Marriage was the last thing on his mind. Then why in the hell did he no longer find the idea of marriage as offending as he had done before?

All he wanted to do now was to pick her up and take her to bed before ravishing her from head to…

"Will you two stop staring at each other?"

With sarcasm dripping, Christina felt like an outsider. It wasn't as if she didn't know that she was beautiful; it was just that she didn't think that she was needed here any more. She knew why Arman had called her and it made her feel rather cynical about this whole thing called love. Although there was no love lost between them, being a woman she did have some fancy views about it. She had hoped that one day Arman would propose to her.

"I'll pack my bags," she announced, trying to keep her emotions at bay and turning her back on them.

"I'll help you," Arman said, his voice abrupt and as devoid of emotions as Christina's was.

6

Arman felt outraged as he felt he could no longer handle her.

"I had been asking her to leave..."

Lifting a brow haughtily, Ria shook her head, "I didn't see her leaving. I rather think you were busy kissing her..."

"*I* didn't kiss her," he replied promptly.

At least he wasn't denying it, she thought with an angry sigh, "*Of course*!"

"Ria...," he walked a step threateningly towards her, "she must have felt awful."

And you think I didn't? Ria wanted to ask. "And what would you have told my parents about bringing your Christina home? That she was your friend?"

Arman shrugged, "Of course."

"And they would have believed you? You don't know my Dad then."

Incredulous eyes stared back at him and Arman wanted to shrug off again, but all he could do was feel stupid. "It was a bad idea, right?"

"Very bad idea, Arman," she said, walking past him. But Aman was quicker for he caught hold of her arm in a tight grip, "Where are you going?"

"To talk to Dad about this whole thing…I have had enough of humiliation to last a lifetime," Ria said, turning her head and looking straight in his eyes. "And I have had enough of men like you."

"Men like me?"

"Men like you who never want to be committed."

Raising his brows in surprise, Arman unconsciously increased the pressure on her arm. She bit her lower lip as he asked severely, "Exactly what kind of commitment do you want? Marriage? *I'm* engaged to you. It *is* you who doesn't want to be married, my dear…it is you who wants to break off. So tell me now, who doesn't want to be committed?"

"*Shut up*!"

"I can't shut up when people make uncalled remarks about me."

Ria tried to pull her arm away as she enunciated each word through her clenched teeth, "Then what did you have with Christina exactly? Were you planning to *marry* her?"

"Damn it!" he jerked her around and the movement was so sudden that Ria slipped and moved closer to him, with his nose touching her upturned head. Ria literally began to tremble. Trying to control herself, Ria glared back at him, but he continued holding her before saying through clenched teeth, "You have been brought up in New York all your life and *such* old fashioned views?"

"It's all the same, Arman. If I had been modern enough, I would have eloped long ago with a nerd who would have wanted to sit on my father's head for all the inheritance."

"So you are saying I'm not a nerd...," said Arman, a grin spreading on his lips, "and that I'm not going to sit on your father's head?"

"Whatever you are Arman Gupta...I don't like you."

"Then what kind of a man do you think I am Ria?"

Narrowing her eyes, Ria's eyelids flickered as those grey eyes sparkled with mischievous humour, "Arrogant, too full of yourself, selfish, heartless..."

"Careful Ria...," his grin faded slowly. "Your hand still belongs to me..."

"I'll see that it never does!"

"I think I have to do something with that sharp tongue of yours as it doesn't stop ever."

"What can *you*..."

Arman growled softly, totally irritated with the entire situation and lowered his head to plant his lips on hers just for the heck of it. This woman could drive a man to the drink, he thought! What he felt was entirely different though...

Her lips were full which he knew they would be. He had touched them the first day that he had met her and she hadn't even moved. It was almost as if she had enjoyed being touched by him...

Without thinking, his arms enveloped her within and she stiffened. Trying to coax her to respond, trying to convince himself that she couldn't affect him, Arman rubbed his lips against hers. He was close to exploding when he felt the softness of her body, which had been exactly as he had expected it to be like.

Then she began to pull herself back and he knew that he wanted her to kiss him. He couldn't force anything on her; least of all, himself. He had never felt like that before...

"*Arman*!" Ria pulled back roughly, almost hurting herself in the process.

The next thing Arman felt was a sharp slap stinging his right cheek. His eyes widened and he glared at Ria, pulling on her shoulder and jerking her roughly, "What was that for?"

"I told you not to touch me!" she almost yelled.

"You think you affect me, don't you?" he felt himself go wild with each word. "You think your telling me not to touch you would make me desperate? A plain little thing like you could do nothing to my libido...!"

With that he pushed her away and stormed out of the hall, his body afire inside out, though he was unwilling to accept the fact. A shadow moved back into the study, having witnessed the entire episode with a bewildered look in his eyes.

* * * * *

"I'm terminating our contract."

Jeevan Gupta jumped from his chair and stared incredulously at the receiver, "I think there must be some kind of a network problem, Amitab. I think I heard..."

"You heard right. I'm terminating our contract..."

"But the designs are almost ready, Amitab. They are undergoing the final processing. Calm down and tell me what's wrong? You just can't terminate..."

Jeevan heard a harsh sigh from the other end, "It's your son. You can call him back by the way."

Jeevan asked hesitantly, "What did Arman do?"

"First he brings his girlfriend home so that he can sleep with her, *then* he kisses my daughter...!" as he said these words, the pitch of his voice increased with every word that he uttered.

Jeevan swallowed hard, "That doesn't sound like Arman. He wouldn't do a thing like that at *your* house."

"Whatever it is, I want him to leave. I don't want him to marry my daughter any more."

"Amitab, calm down...," Jeevan began, knowing how stubborn Amitab could be.

"Will it matter if I calm down?" Amitab Melhera demanded.

"Uh...yes."

"No it would not..." Amitab felt just short of pulling his hair out when he heard the door of his study open. He shaded his eyes when he saw his daughter come in. "I'll talk to you later," he mumbled as he put the phone down.

"Dad...," Ria's voice was filled with anger, instead of the tears he thought he would be seeing.

"What is it, Ria?"

"I don't want to..."

"Marry Arman?" he completed for her with a tilt of his eyebrows.

Ria blew away a strand of air from her eyes and shook

her head, "I wanted to say I don't want to stay here any more. I don't belong here and..."

"Wait, you just lost me."

"I told you from the start that I can't stay here forever..."

"Is this a way to avoid something or someone, Ria?"

Ria narrowed her eyes, "By any mistake are you sure you are not my biological father?"

"What?"

"No, I mean how do you know whatever goes on in my mind?"

Biting his cheeks from laughing out aloud, Amitab said, "Tell me what you want to tell me, Ria..."

"But you never listen to me and decide all by yourself what's best for me!"

"Okay, this time I will listen."

Ria stared suspiciously at him, "Okay, I don't want to..."

The door behind her creaked open and they both heard Arman's voice, "Can I come in?"

"Yes."

"No!" Ria shouted at the same time.

"I'm coming *in* anyways," Arman answered back rudely.

"Yeah sure...*do* what you want...just as you always do!" Ria snapped.

"I don't *do* anything until I'm instigated!"

"You two can stop that now," Amitab said, rolling his eyes and waiting till they both faced him. "What's bothering you both?"

"He is!"

"She is!"

They said together.

He leaned back comfortably on the chair and nodded his head, "That's not news. I already know that. Now what do you think I should do?" Before they could open their mouths, he continued, "I'm breaking off your engagement. You two don't have to bear each other any more."

"Breaking *off*...?" Ria stared at her father blankly.

"What do you mean...?" They turned to look at each other and stopped abruptly.

"Fine," Amitab Melhera said in a tired voice, "I'll have your ticket booked for tomorrow, Arman."

"You don't bother about that Mr Melhera," Arman said smilingly, "as I have already booked my ticket. I needed to talk about the finished designs." He paused and his eyes turned unyielding, "I got a call from my Dad."

"What contract?" Ria asked confusedly, her mind a bit hazy with the knowledge that she wasn't engaged any more.

"Just a business, sweetheart," Amitab answered pleasantly. "I'll talk to you later, okay?"

"Is that a sweet way of asking me to get out?"

"You are not to involve yourself in this, Ria," Arman's hard voice stopped her from saying anything more.

'Men!' Ria just shook her head in dismay. They don't want any involvement when it comes to serious discussions.

After Ria had left the room, Arman glared at Mr Melhera, trying desperately not to show his anger at his highhandedness. This man had turned his life upside down!

"Just what do you mean by terminating..."

"Look Arman...," Amitab leaned forward in his chair, a

little restless. "I know that your company and mine would have been great together but I just cannot put my daughter's happiness at stake!"

"Since when did personal happiness come into business, Mr Melhera?" Arman asked, walking towards Amitab's desk and thumping it with both his hands. "I never was sure about this engagement. You forced me, my father forced me and now that I'm trying to come to terms with this farce, you break the engagement! Just what in the hell do you think my life is?"

Amitab's brows rose at each word, "I was not sure either. Maybe it was just an excuse to keep my daughter away from womanisers…"

"*Really*? Then you have failed Mr Melhera! Your daughter is in love with someone and that someone is married!"

As soon as the words left his lips, Arman regretted it from his heart and soul. This was something that he wasn't supposed to tell Ria's parents of all the people! Damn it, why couldn't he just control his temper? And why in the hell was he still bothered about the fact that Ria was in love with a married guy? He should have been more concerned about the contract he was about to lose!

"Just what in the *hell* do you mean by that?" Amitab Melhera snapped, his eyes no longer amused.

"Look, I didn't…"

"Did Ria tell you that?" Amitab's voice was not prepared to hear any argument. "What is that bastard's name?"

"I don't know his name," Arman moved back and buried his hands into his pockets, "and you weren't supposed to know since you don't seem to have any knowledge about Ria's lover…"

"*Lover*!" Amitab yelled. "I think I'm going to have a heart attack!"

Arman seriously doubted *that*. He just stared for a long moment at the distraught father and understandably so. He shrugged lightly, "She was living in New York and you can't blame her if she blended with that culture."

Amitab gnashed his teeth and stared hard at Arman, "This is why exactly I had got her engaged when she was sixteen!"

"I didn't know I was engaged either, so…"

"Do you want the contract, Arman?" Amitab cut short the conversation with a wave of his hand.

"Of course!" he got to the point. "We have been slogging our butts to reach this stage!"

"I don't care a damn about your hard work!" Amitab said, sounding like a true businessman now. "But if it means a lot to you, then marry my daughter or lose everything!"

* * * * *

The door closed behind Ria and she stood uncertainly for a second, staring at nothing in particular. She felt odd regarding her engagement that she had been forced to withstand for the past one week. Not that she wanted to be engaged to Arman, she tried to convince herself, since they were no match. Arman deserved someone beautiful and as interesting as him.

Since when had she thought that he *was* interesting? Shaking her head in confusion, she walked towards the dining room, hoping that the feeling of doom would soon pass away. She was no longer engaged to Arman and she didn't have to bear him any more.

She didn't have to hide it any more...and she didn't have to tell anyone how she felt.

7

"Marry *my daughter or lose...!*"Arman kept on repeating it until he reached his room and sat down on the bed, rubbing his forehead while nursing the first headache of his life.

"Both the daughter and father are insane!" he told himself with a sigh, 'First I had to marry her to please my Dad and now I have to marry her to please my company and that old bastard!'

"I won't marry her!" he yelled to himself. "I don't have to please anyone!"

He turned swiftly towards his suitcase and began to dump his clothes without precision. This was one deranged trip that he should have never taken. Everything had been so confusing and when he was almost close to breaking off the engagement, he was being blackmailed into it now – and that too with his company's future at stake! Damn it, he had worked really hard to see it succeed. He just couldn't let it go this way...

But marriage…

Just then the balcony door opened and he saw Ria come out of her room, wearing her nightdress. It wasn't the sexy kind he thought women usually preferred but a long T-shirt that touched her knees and white bunny shoes that made her feet look like two rabbits, ready to flee. The breeze touched her and passed her way back and forth, blowing her soft hair hither and thither. Again he felt the same stirrings of hunger that he always felt whenever he saw her. What was this? It had to be lust, he thought a bit cynically. She was a woman whom any man would want to bed, hold, *love*…

Stop right there, Arman! And which he did. He saw a smile curving on her lips – lips that could kill him any day. Why did he feel that way about her? She didn't like him to even touch her. Did she feel repulsed by his touch? Just the idea sent a chill down his spine. She couldn't be repulsed, for sure! He wasn't a man who could take it from a woman he desired so badly that he almost ached with it.

He wanted her, he realised dismally. Of all the women, he had to want her!

He had the chance to make love to Christina that morning but he could not respond. Damn, he hadn't even felt anything at her touch.

Ria turned and pushed her hair away from her face. Her face was devoid of any makeup, yet it glowed as always. Maybe they needed to talk after all…

Or maybe he wanted to just stand beside her and enjoy her fragrance…

Without thinking much, Arman slipped out of the room to go outside and went and stood beside her. At first he thought she hadn't noticed or realised that he was standing beside her, but after a minute had passed, he realised that she was ignoring him!

Damn it, this woman was a tough cookie!

"Aren't you going to say something?"

"I don't want to spoil my mood by talking to you," she replied sharply.

"Has anyone told you what a bitch you are, Ria?"

That caught her attention and she turned to look at him, her eyes shadowed and her curls falling over her eyes again, "Yeah."

Something twisted in his heart and his anger suddenly erupted, "Who called you...?"

"His wife," she replied without any emotions. Turning to look at the dark night, she added, "Now don't start asking me questions."

"I guess I don't have the right to ask," he agreed softly, feeling absurdly comfortable with her.

There was a moment of silence between them when suddenly Ria felt Arman's hands across her shoulders. The touch startled her so much that she shivered.

"I'm sorry," she heard him say.

"For what?" she tried to sound calm and take her mind off his touch.

The hold tightened, so she gave up thinking altogether, "No one has the right to call you names; not even me. So next time if I do it, you can hit me on my face and I won't squeak even."

"I...I did hit you today."

She felt his hand move away and felt a moment of loss.

Why couldn't he keep on touching her? It felt so good and comforting.

No, she didn't want to feel that...she didn't want to feel desired! And Arman did say that he didn't desire her. She didn't do anything for his libido...yes, that's what he had said!

"Because I kissed you."

"Why did you kiss me?"

Because you are kissable, he wanted to say, but he just tightened his hands on the railing in front of him.

"You make me angry."

"You grabbed me," she returned. "What was I supposed to do?"

Again silence.

Curious, Ria looked at Arman. He looked tense, standing there. His hair was as usual tied and for a change he was not wearing his glasses. He didn't look any different. In fact she didn't think she resented his glasses that much. He did look kind of distinguished in whatever he wore, even in a loose T-shirt and brown khakis. She couldn't forget what she had glimpsed inside them. Gosh, why couldn't she forget the way he looked without clothes?

"You make me angrier than any woman does, Ria," he justified himself carefully. "And I have a devil of a time controlling my words. They keep rolling...and then..."

"Then you regret?"

His head whipped around and his eyes sparkled, "I didn't regret kissing you."

"But you said I didn't do anything for your libido..."

His hands caught her arm in a tight grip and his other

hand pushed away those curls off her eyes. Looking up into those eyes, Ria felt a drowning sensation. His hands felt hard and strong and even though his grip was firm, it didn't hurt. In fact, it felt good to be held like that.

"Are you going to kiss me?" she whispered, as if telling him a secret.

A smile curved on his lips, "I think you *want* me to....," he said, bending and whispering into her ears and rolling the tip of his tongue along with his words.

The words took her by surprise and Ria wanted to say 'yes'. It was the perfect moment to kiss and he felt so good in her arms. He was solid and safe...

Not like...her eyes suddenly filled with tears and a drop fell.

When she felt the brush of his lips, she felt him stiffen. "You are crying," Arman said, watching the play of emotions cross over her face. He touched a fingertip to her trembling lips and then another tear fell, followed by another... "*Damn it,* you loved him so much that you can't even bear me to touch you?"

Her eyes flew and she started to shiver, "I don't want to talk about him!"

"Yes, you do!" he growled, not letting her move. "I can see that it's eating you inside. I might not be your favourite person right now Ria, but you've got to talk about this."

"There is nothing to talk!" she tried to jerk her arms away but failed unsuccessfully.

"Talk to me Ria...," his voice was almost pleading. "I hate to see you this way."

A pathetic wail escaped from her lips and he swore softly,

pulling her into his arms tightly. "Shush! Don't cry…I'm here. If you don't want to talk, I won't force you…"

"He said nothing about being married. I didn't know!" she said and although Arman could hardly comprehend what she was saying, because of her continuous sobs, he let her talk without interrupting. "He…he just thought I would conveniently forget about a wife in the background. I…I wanted to kill him so much. But all I did was avoid him. I couldn't even tell him what a scoundrel he had been. I thought I loved him so much…why couldn't I see the signs?…Why couldn't I! Why was I such a fool?"

"Everybody is a fool in love," he tried to joke, but failed miserably. All he did was to make her cry harder.

Sighing, Arman held her closer still. He tried not to think how perfect her body felt, how soft she was and how he wanted to carry her to the closest thing to bed her and make love to her…

"I'm sorry," she managed to draw those words out before pulling herself away.

He didn't stop her because all his energy had been sapped out somewhere between his legs. He stood stiffly, wanting her to kiss him and make love to him…God he wanted her so much!

"You should sleep," he said softly.

She nodded, trying to hide from him her embarrassment. "I just want you to know that he doesn't affect me any more. It was more of a blow to my ego than to my heart, but…"

Arman was beginning to feel better with her words when that 'but' of her annoyed him. "But what?"

"But I still believe in love, Arman. I would marry only

for love!" she said, turning to leave towards her room. On reaching the doorstep, her parting shot was, "And it's a good thing that we are no longer engaged because I don't love you."

* * * * *

That night, as expected, Arman couldn't sleep. May be he had been idle for too long. Suddenly he was forced to think about marriage and stuff. And he really wasn't interested... *right?*

He rolled over to the empty side of the bed and sighed loudly. He was twenty-eight, for God's sake! He was at least supposed to be sure about his personal life. What was happening to him? It was not as if it was the end of the world, was it? And on top of that, his professional life was going to be messed up because of that. And all because he wasn't getting married to Ria.

Ria. He closed his eyes and found himself having a headache. He could never be sure of her. Why did she have to cry like that in front of him? And why in the hell was he feeling like getting up right now and go to her?

Lust? That's what it was. And after all, lust just does fade away. He just didn't have to see her, meet her and feel her...gradually he would forget her. Yes, that's what he was going to do. Somehow the thought made his heartbeat increase and a hollow feeling began to form inside him.

Turning over on his back, he groaned with a defeated sigh, 'Oh God...I have got to marry her!'

The next evening Ria sent and stood at the edge of her terrace and watch the day turn into night. Her mind was crowded with all kinds of thoughts. The evening had already faded and she had a hard frown on her forehead as she tried not to think of the night gone by. She wasn't supposed to cry that way in front of him…and especially *him*! But she could not restrain herself from thinking about the way his arms held her; it seemed as if he cared for how she felt.

Yeah right! Pigs would start flying when he would start caring. If he had really cared about her feelings, then he wouldn't have brought his girlfriend home and planned to sleep with her to break off their engagement.

And since morning he had been out, and she couldn't ask anyone about his whereabouts. Maybe he had already left, she assumed.

The view was magnificent from the terrace. There was just so much of lush greenery that just looking at the colour gave her so much peace of mind. That was how she had felt when she was in his arms…She closed her eyes and admonished herself for thinking about Arman's arms, of all the things!

"Ria?" she heard her name being called out.

She didn't have to turn and guess whose voice it was. Why in the hell did he follow her wherever she was?

"I'm not following you, okay?"

"Then, what are you doing here? I thought you would be busy packing and gone already."

"I'm not going anywhere," he asserted, raising his brows and displaying conviction. He went and stood right beside her, but she didn't want to look at him. Nevertheless, it was not easy to ignore his presence. His personality was so magnetic that his scent was overpowering. He looked fresh as if he had just taken a shower. No wonder that musky smell was intoxicating!

"Dad asked you to leave...," she began, "and you said you had your tickets booked."

"What would you say if I tell you we are still engaged?"

8

"What!?" Ria whirled around, her eyes suddenly inflamed. "Dad broke it up."

Arman hesitated, seeing the beginnings of confusion in her eyes. Then he began to think of a logical way to put this whole thing together. He said, "He just can't break and fix us up whenever he wants, right?"

She opened her mouth to argue, but he shook his head, "You know what I mean."

"But…"

"Why do you keep adding so many 'buts'?"

Ria pursed her lips, "Because this is a situation where I can't be left to wonder what would really happen!"

"Have you ever wondered why the sun rises and why it sets?"

Ria turned a frowned look at Arman, "No…I just admire

the beauty and anyway, it's an odd question."

Arman hid a smile and nodded, "Precisely. You don't question the why's and how's of beauty, Ria. You just admire it. Then why do you need to worry so much about our marriage?"

"Arman...," Ria sighed softly and the slump of her shoulders should have made him feel guilty, but he did not seem concerned. "I'm not related to the sun...but after our marriage, *I'm* going to be related to you."

"You are right. But would it be so bad to be related to me?"

Casting him a bemused look, Ria mumbled, "No."

In fact she didn't think she would ever regret marrying him. Arman was every woman's dream man. He was perfect the way he looked and perhaps another woman would have been happier to be landed with him. Today he sounded different; almost sensible. In fact, she thought with a grimace, Arman was always sensible about everything – even when he had suggested that she could go her own way and end their engagement. She hadn't thought then that it would matter to her but after seeing Arman and Christina together, she knew that she couldn't let any woman have him.

It had to be her!

"You are wondering about love again, right?"

"No...yes!...*uhhh*...," said Ria, shaking her head, her mind jumbled with all kinds of thoughts – Arman and Christina, she and Arman, their impending marriage and their future.

"You don't have to worry about that, you know," Arman said as if reading her thoughts. "I have never been in love and as far as I know, you haven't *actually* been in love either. We could learn to love each other."

Ria narrowed her eyes and wanted to say that his statement sounded very Victorian and *boring*. What could 'learn to love each other' mean? Was she not loveable enough now? Couldn't he just fall right on his feet and tell her that he loved her? Just like that, without citing any reason?

But that would be foolhardy.

"I want love right *now*," she gritted her teeth stubbornly.

Behind her she heard Arman take a sharp, impatient breath before grasping her firmly by the shoulders, "Why is it that you are obsessed with love? Do you know that love fizzles away while fondness would remain?"

"I could make do with love," she added after a moment of thinking.

"Damn!"

Ria didn't know that she could smile over her meeting with Christina. Now she wanted to laugh. Good, let him simmer and let him wonder!

"So you are going to say 'yes' after I confess I love you?"

Ria turned then, her eyes no longer watching the dipping sun but the intense emotions in Arman's eyes. What was wrong with him today? The way he had dressed today didn't look as immaculate and his hair wasn't tied either. She didn't know why but she felt her heart beat faster at that rakish look of his. She felt her heart take a somersault. Would love matter that much?

Maybe not…maybe…

"Okay, let's pretend that we are in love," she heard him say.

"*What?*"

"I said...," began Arman, taking a deep breath, straighttening himself and looking down at her with impassive features, "Let's pretend we love each other..."

"And?"

"I'll propose," he continued and for a moment Ria thought he was going to turn and run away from all this.

But there he stood, right in front of her, so tall and so handsome, yet so arrogant!

"I don't care for proposals," she said flippantly.

"Okay, you can propose then," he added quickly and blinked when Ria laughed.

"*Yeah*, right!"

"I'm serious Ria. Either you propose or I will."

Her hands dropped to her hips as if worried. She demanded, "Why is it so important for you? I'm not even good looking and I don't own my Dad's money...Why is it that you want to marry me?"

Because I can't resist you – it was almost on Arman's lips to tell her that but he remained quiet, knowing well enough that Ria was not in the mood to hear that. She wanted to hear the words '*I love you*' and if they meant so much to her, then he was prepared to say them, even though he wasn't sure of the kind of love they were supposed to have.

"You propose," she said and he saw another confused look enter her eyes.

Arman went down on his knees and Ria gasped when she saw him holding her hands in his. She marvelled at the way he hid any discomfiture he might have felt at having to do this. He looked so comfortable and content to be doing it.

"Have you done this before?"

"Only in front of God," he answered quietly.

Ria felt the significance of his words and for a moment felt her entire body fill with pleasure. At that moment she almost felt close to loving Arman. And the way his eyes changed colour made her want to kiss them and tell him she was his…she didn't need any damn proposal from him.

Arman, taking a deep breath and looking right into her eyes, said, "Ria, I love you." The words somehow felt right on his tongue though she could have never known how damn scared he felt right then. "I never thought how life would have been if I hadn't met you. I know that we are not perfect individuals, but I find you flawless. I don't care what you think about me right now…," he suddenly found himself grinning. "Most probably you think I'm a fool, but I don't care."

"Okay *stop*!" Ria said, trembling from head to foot, and running her fingers to push her curls away from her eyes.

She turned to leave and end the farce, when he called out, "Wait!"

"Why?" she didn't turn around.

"I thought we were going to pretend love."

"That was your sick idea," Ria said, feeling compelled to point it out.

"Ria, please…," Arman begged.

Please? Why did he say that? He had never begged to anyone in his life and now he was begging to her to marry him? How desperate could he get?

But his hands moved automatically and caught her by her waist. She was trembling he realised and felt his heart tug.

All thoughts of his own desperation faded to give way to genuine concern.

"Let me go," her voice didn't sound too steady.

"You are trembling," he voiced uncertainly.

"It's cold out here…I'm cold."

"You are not," he pulled her closer to him with a jerk and groaned with pleasure and pain.

"Arman…what…"

"You are so hot, Ria. I touch you and I…," his lips grazed the top of her forehead and she felt her tremble more. "I think I go up in flames when I touch you. You are the only one who affects me this way, Ria. I want to share my bed with you…to make love to you and make you happy."

"Was…was that a pretence too?"

Turning her around with the same swiftness, Arman glared angrily at her. He was angry? Whatever emotion she had expected, Ria had never thought of seeing him angry at her words, "Do you think what I feel is pretence? *Ria, I want you badly;* so badly that I don't even want to wait for our marriage vows. I don't want to reach for the bed to touch you. I don't want to *wait,* Ria!"

"Oh God, I hate you Arman. I hate you!" she wailed and began to sob.

Arman didn't know how he was to react. She had always been rude to him but this helplessness was not like her. Was he imposing himself too much on her? Should he back out?

He felt her head slowly drop on his chest and he stopped breathing. She was crying quite pathetically and his hands reached to hold the curl at the back of her head and slowly turn her to face up at him. Staring at those sparkling eyes brimming with haunting tears, Arman didn't realise what he was doing when he bent to kiss her.

He wished she had pushed him away or slapped him just as she had done the previous time, but as soon as his lips touched hers, her lips clung to his. This time he felt he was nearly dead. God, she tasted so sweet and so heavenly? So soft and *so*…

His hands tightened and disappeared into her thick mane. Just touching them was to make his other wish come true. Even the last time when he had touched her, he had wanted more. He wanted to wrap his hands around her hair and bury his face in them. The kiss turned sizzling and almost carnal. Arman knew the art of kissing but kissing Ria then had nothing to do with art; it had to do with desire, and want, and yearning!

Her body drew closer but he couldn't fit her close enough. Moving his hands down to her buttocks, he shifted her closer. The organ of his desire jumped at the friction and he traced his tongue on hers.

Suddenly they were pushing each other away. Breathing heavily as if they had run a marathon, both stared at each other suspiciously. Arman's suspicion was based upon her passionate response and Ria's suspicion was directed at her own impulsiveness and Arman's sudden desire for her.

"Were you going to stop?" Ria hissed, her eyes spitting fire but her body sizzling with his touch.

"Were you?" Arman spat back.

No, Ria realised heavily. She didn't want to stop. She did not want to stop ever.

"So, now will you marry me?"

Agitated at his question, she realised that he knew what was going on in her mind. "Okay…but…"

The triumphant look in Arman's eyes made words die abruptly on her lips and Ria swallowed, "But…"

"But?"

Ria threw a challenging look at him, "You and I don't pretend love. If you don't love me, then don't. I'll just leave you if you do that again." She snapped her thumb and middle finger together, "Just like that and I won't look back."

Arman's mouth tightened at that and suddenly he didn't feel like.

"We will see who leaves first!"

Ria didn't like hearing those words, "I'm serious, Arman."

"Don't worry, Ria, you are never going to hear the word *love* from my lips again!"

This was not what Ria wanted to hear either.

* * * * *

"You are finally getting married to him then?" Tanvi asked, picking up a book, though all her concentration was entirely upon Ria's pale features.

"Yes."

"Arman forced you?"

"He can't force anything on me, Tanvi. You take *that* from me!"

Tanvi's brows rose and her smile was almost comical. "I never thought you would marry him, but I guess Dad left you with no choice."

"He looks damn happy," Ria muttered, still feeling betrayed over the fact that he hadn't really broken their engagement. Maybe he had done it just to see her happy! But was she happy, really happy when she had heard that they didn't have to get married?

"You know Ria, you have no reason to look so glum," Tanvi continued cheerfully. "Arranged marriages happen all the time and some people even choose it..."

"You make it sound like some kind of punishment," Ria returned glumly.

"Well...," Tanvi laughed a little nervously, "marriage is not a bed of roses. You think love is easy to handle Ria, but you have to work on every relationship to make it work..."

"But being in love makes it easier, I guess."

Shrugging her shoulders and feeling helpless, Tanvi nodded, "I guess so."

"I don't love him."

"You can't always think about that man," her cousin walked out of her room. "Grow up, Ria. Life is offering you something better."

"Tanvi!" Ria called out, her voice a little desperate. "I...don't know what to do."

Tanvi faltered at the door and then turned, "Take a chance. He is a dangerous man with whom you could fall seriously in love! And what more can a wife want than to be in love with her husband?"

* * * * *

"That woman is a pain in the butt!" Arman growled as he walked back and forth in his room. "I go and put my heart and soul in front of her and all she does is to click fingers in front of me!"

The knock on his door made him want to pull the door out of its place. Why in the hell did he agree to come here in the first place? He wouldn't have ever met Ria and there wouldn't have been any desire in him for her. But this wouldn't do. She should never know how she affected him…

He gritted his teeth, almost hurting his jaw. *She did know how he felt about her and she was going to take advantage of it* – of that he was sure. As far as he knew women, they always did take advantage of how their men felt about them.

"Arman!" he heard Ria's voice and he rolled his eyes. *Think of the devil…!*

"What do you want?"

There was a pause and when he thought she had gone, there was another knock. Giving up, he wrenched the door open and glared at her, "What is it?"

With her hands on her hips, Ria raised a brow, "Is that the way to talk to your future wife?"

"Get used to it," he told her sweetly.

The raised brow didn't move an inch, "Fine! If you think that handsome face of yours would make me submissive, then think again, mister!"

The scowl on his face deepened, "Why are you here? I need my privacy."

"Just came to tell you that Dad is holding a private get-together in the evening. He would be announcing our engagement officially. So you are supposed to be ready on time."

"That would just be extending the entire thing. Why not just get married?"

"Unfortunately it's not an occasion of mourning for my family as it is for us. I could have reacted the same way, but Dad is not prepared to listen to me."

"You don't really know how to convince your Dad," Arman said, relishing his words.

This time Ria looked really agitated, "And I really don't appreciate you behaving like a spoilt child, Arman..."

"Me? A *spoilt* child?" he moved a step forward. "Do I look like a child to you?"

"A spoilt one," she raised her chin, her eyes sparkling bright. "And I'm not going to reach that height of yours. You always behave as if it's my fault."

"To remind you with all due respect, you were the one who behaved like a spoilt child when I arrived...," Arman's eyes flickered and she took a step forward this time. "And when I'm trying to be as civil as possible with you, you are calling me a spoilt child! *You* are most selfish, most arrogant yourself, Miss Ria Melhera and you have no right to call me one!"

"Have you finished?"

Arman just couldn't bear it any more. If she was going to behave this way, then she would have to improve on her finishing lines. "Well...there is one more thing."

"What?" she asked tartly.

His arms pulled her tightly against him and his lips moved hard on hers. "This!" he said against her mouth.

Ria eyes widened in shock as she savoured the feel of his lips. The kiss was intensely passionate yet...brief?

"Well, tell your Dad that I'll be ready," he said without meeting her eyes and she saw the door close with a loud bang.

"You look horrible," Ria said with relish, though she wanted to bite her tongue for telling such a lie. In fact she expected the lightning to strike her right then and there.

Arman tipped his head to one side and whispered softly into her ears, deliberately letting his lips linger, "You too, sweetheart."

Ria's breath caught at the endearment and she quickly looked away. Arman looked anything but horrible that night. Wearing a fitted black Armani suit, he oozed sex appeal that could make any woman fall for him! That reminded her how he could still want to marry her. His hair was combed back and shone with dynamic effect. His jaw, clean shaven, looked so inviting that she wished she could plant a kiss on it. He wasn't wearing his glasses and his eyes looked mysterious than ever. And when it met hers, she blinked back a sigh…

She was going to get engaged to this gorgeous man! She wanted to hoot, she wanted to yell…and she wanted to cry.

This man was really dangerous – the way he had proposed to her, made her want to fall for him and indeed she had fallen…almost.

Arman avoided looking at Ria whenever they were together. There were a lot of people around and he didn't know most of them. But everyone he met was good natured and friendly. He accepted their good wishes wholeheartedly, when all he wanted to do was to get away from all this and go back home.

As he turned around next, he noticed Ria talking to another young woman who looked very obviously pregnant.

The young woman looked like she didn't belong to the glamorous high society, yet she had an austerity on her face that was attractive. But when he looked at Ria, he found her to be the most beautiful woman and what was more, she looked radiant for a woman who was unhappy with her marriage. Sighing, he saw Mr Melhera join them with a purpose to complete the ring ceremony.

'Okay, I'm ready,' he muttered to himself.

"I'm so glad you came...," Ria gushed, hardly containing her excitement.

"I just came to wish you...Rumán would be mad at me if he learns that I came to meet my parents."

Ria's brow knitted with concern, "But they are busy hiding themselves from you. You shouldn't have eloped Monica..."

"Not you too! I met Mom secretly" Monica grinned. "It's complicated, but we are very happy, Ria. And he loves me very much," she added, moving forward to whisper naughtily, "He is a great lover too."

"*Monica*!" Ria laughed, grinning at her. "No wonder you are pregnant...and looking beautiful too."

Blushing, Monica shrugged her shoulders, "Now that you are getting married soon...I'll be waiting for the good news too, Ria."

"What good news?" Arman chimed in as he joined them, smiling charmingly at the young woman.

"When Ria would be looking just like me," Monica replied with a smile, running her palms softly on her stomach.

Ria closed her eyes, swallowing a lump of embarrassment. She didn't even want to look at Arman and how he would have taken it. It was a good thing too because he looked shocked and suddenly pleased at the prospect of having a baby with Ria.

Ria wanted to curse. Of all the things, she didn't expect Arman to look pleased! That would be the day when she would be pregnant with Arman's baby.

"I'll be glad to put her in this position," Arman returned with a twinkle in his eye.

"*What?*"

"The rings!" her father came in between, "Monica… Monica?" his eyes moved down her body before moving to her laughing, "Oh my God! What…when…?"

"I got married last year, uncle."

"You must be…you are too young," he said confusedly.

"Not that," Monica argued.

"She is nineteen, Dad…," Ria tried to defend her friend, "and she is out of the cradle…She can bear a child."

"Of course."

"We are glad you came," Arman tried to take control of the awkward situation.

"I left home on my eighteenth birthday to escape from Dad's thrashing…"

"Why would he trash you?" Arman asked curiously.

"I married an outcast who is still slogging his butt for me. Dad thinks it's a *big* sin…," Monica noticed the colour drain from Ria's father's face and swallowed a laugh. Amitab Melhera was among those who always felt that he had a place in society because he maintained his dignity. Maybe just to avoid all the embarrassment of a daughter who chose a useless man as her husband, he had deliberately taken the matters in his own hands. And he was going to succeed.

"Shall we start the engagement ceremony?" Vidhya joined them.

"Uh…yes."

Ria shot daggers at her father and moved away with Arman.

"I don't know why he behaves like that," Ria muttered.

"He is not bad; he wasn't warned about it…"

"He just wants to run people's lives…he should understand that he is not the only one with brains…!"

Arman's fingers brushed against her arms, "Don't…this is your engagement party. Look happy."

Ria looked up and at his eyes. Sighing deeply, she nodded and stretched her lips wide into a smile, "Don't I look happy?"

"It comes from within…but I guess I can't force anything on you."

"That's right…not even yourself!"

Rolling his eyes heavenward, Arman gave her a gritty smile, thinking…*and here she goes again…*

The ring ceremony was a sober one and everyone was enjoying except for Ria and Arman. When Arman slipped in the ring on her ring finger, Ria didn't look up. Her eyes were fixed on the ring embedded with diamonds and sapphires. It was a beautiful ring. She slipped a gold one with three diamonds in the centre on Arman's finger and he too didn't look up either.

What could he be thinking, Ria wondered when back in her room. Tired, she unwrapped the heavy embroidered pink sari and placed it carefully on the bed. Maybe she had overreacted but what in the hell was she supposed to do when Arman started behaving unpredictably?

Like kissing her…

Why did he have to kiss her when she had repeatedly asked him not to? Why did he have to irritate her that way? But it was difficult to forget his words…*I want to share my bed with you…to make love to you and make you happy…*

Could he make her happy?

The big question was whether they could make each other happy…

9

Arman left for New York the next day and Ria came to know about it through Tanvi, who seemed unhappy to be the bearer of the bad news.

"I didn't know he hadn't told you about it," Tanvi said with a deep frown.

Ria shrugged, trying to sound casual, "It's okay…just because we are marrying doesn't mean that I have to rule his life."

"But…"

Ria got up and left, fuming inside. *Just what in the hell did he think of himself!?*

The day passed…and another one passed. Then the whole week went by without a word from him. Ria stayed quiet and sober, trying to pretend that she wasn't missing him.

And she wasn't missing him, she told herself sternly. Amitab Melhera looked at his daughter and thought how hard she looked from outside but so vulnerable within as if she would crack any minute. She didn't even talk to him nowadays, which hurt, but he didn't say much. He wanted her to be happy, though he couldn't stop blaming himself. After all, which daughter would like a marriage being forced on her? Arman was a good guy but only too impulsive for his own good!

"Did you find out about the colleges around here for…," he began speaking in order to break the ice.

But she interrupted him rudely, "What's the use? You are getting me married and I'm going back to New York again!" she got up from the dining table, walked straight into her room and locked herself in, cursing under her breath.

"She looks unhappy," Vidhya commented under her breath, glaring at her husband.

"That's because she misses Arman," Amitab said with a grin, but failed to convince his wife.

"And pigs fly!" Vidhya snapped.

Amitab winced and shook his head, "She is engaged to him."

"She *was* engaged long back, Amitab! What's changed is that now she *knows* about it and it's making her damn unhappy!"

Wincing, Amitab nodded his head, "Arman has to be back very soon…"

"That he has to be!" Vidhya muttered, "or you have to send Ria back."

"I don't mind," Amitab said getting up from the table. "In fact I think I'll do just that."

"*Amitab*! I was kidding!"

Shrugging, Amitab Melhera flipped his mobile and started dialling numbers in a frenzy, "I'll send her on pretence, or else she wouldn't go."

"Don't start that again!"

Raising a brow Amitab, "That's right, Vidhya...*I'm* going to start this again and this time in the very right way. No harm spending some time together now, is there?"

* * * * *

"You are shipping me off to New York!" Ria fumed, "and can I ask why should I go there to bring those stupid files you left at home...? Seriously Dad, it is the *lamest* excuse I have ever heard in my whole life!"

Amitab grinned sheepishly, "I thought you wanted to go back..."

"That I still do, but not for your files! I'm least interested in your business!"

"True," Amitab agreed. "If you would have shown a little interest in it, I guess I never would have thought about getting you married," he sighed as he sat down, slumping his shoulders as if he had aged and was unable to carry the burden.

Groaning softly, Ria sat down beside her father, "Dad, you thought life in a foreign country would spoil me but look, I am all in one piece and I was doing well in my studies. If I had known that you wanted some help, then do you think I would have refused?"

"You never liked business," Amitab pointed out.

"Yeah, I guess changing your profession was never an option?" Ria teased him lightly. It produced a small laugh from him.

"You are a brat, Ria, but always my favourite daughter."

"You don't have a choice. I'm the only one you have!" Ria returned with a grin. "Alright Dad, I'll bring those files for you and I'll even go to your office personally. If you want…"

"Perfect!" Amitab said, the worry in his eyes miraculously disappearing. "You do that!"

Eyeing her Dad suspiciously, Ria nodded nonetheless.

10

It had been a month since he had heard from Ria. He got to hear many things about her, but never got a call from her. If he had thought that she would miss him terribly, then he was mistaken. She still didn't care. This realisation made him so restless that he couldn't concentrate on his work. In truth he had returned abroad to get down to work to avoid any personal interludes with her. And maybe it was working, as it meant he didn't have to talk to her. That was what he wanted and that's what he planned to do henceforth – avoid her!

Leaning back on his chair, he dialled a number, forcing his thoughts away from his fiancée. He shut his mobile. *Fiancée?*

He swallowed hard.

How the hell could he avoid his fiancée? How the hell could he avoid Ria?

He could not forget her luscious body, her soft lips and her sparkling black eyes, piping hot with temper, try as much as he could. And how beautiful she looked when angry! Usually he didn't have the patience or the inclination to stand anyone throwing tantrums, but this woman looked sexy when angry. Suddenly he smiled as he realised that he was missing her. So, he was behaving like a man in love...so what? He knew he wasn't in love, right?

Of course he wasn't...

His mobile rang and he grabbed to pick it up. Maybe it was Ria...

"Wan'na make out tonight?" he heard a sultry voice. His heart skipped a beat. He was so very ready to hear from Ria that he almost imagined Ria telling him those words. Then he heard a giggle and he screwed his face when he recognised the voice. It irked him to know who it was.

"Chris...I thought you were on the move. How come you are back so soon?"

"Oh Arman...I'll be leaving tomorrow again. I just didn't want to spend the night alone..."

"I see," he said in a bored voice, "and may I ask why I have the exclusive pleasure?"

"Come on...I heard you got engaged and it's been so long since we..."

"That's right Chris, I'm engaged and I intend to stay so. You can find another companion for yourself. I don't mind," he said sharply and hung up, sighing loudly to himself.

Shit, he was in love!

All those years of meaningless relationships were getting to his head...he could not be in love. He tried to convince himself again and again.

The mobile rang again and groaning under his breath, he picked it up again, "Yes?" he snapped.

"Ria is coming there," was the first thing he heard from Amitab Melhera's voice.

"*What*?" he jumped from his chair. "You must be kidding, right?"

"Do I ever?"

Rolling his eyes heavenwards, Arman grinned, "I love you, Dad!"

On the other side of the phone, a shocked Amitab Melhera was having laughter fits after a long time in his life.

* * * * *

Ria raised a single brow and did a double take. Was it Arman that she was seeing? What was he doing here at the airport?

Stepping out from the immigration check, Ria tipped her head to her left and narrowed her eyes. He looked nervous and she wondered why. As if she cared, she thought grumpily. It's been a long month and he hadn't called once even after coming here. Maybe Christina was back in his life and he had forgotten all about her. That bothered her a little.

"Hello Ria," she heard him say as she stepped out.

She viewed his empty hands and bit her lower lip, "What are you doing here?"

"Receiving you," he said with a smile that seemed genuine too.

"Who told you I was coming?" she asked, not pretending that she was happy to see him. Just seeing him there was making her blood boil.

"Uh, I came to know," Arman hedged, watching each and every movement of hers. "Aren't you glad to see me?"

"If you think you are doing a favour by receiving me here, then let me inform you Mr Gupta, I have lived here long enough to know my whereabouts...I don't need your assistance!"

Releasing an exasperated breath, Arman took the small suitcase from her and remarked, "You aren't glad to see me – that's what I know."

Ria looked away, her heart pinching when she heard a soft note of regret in Arman's voice. Why was he feeling bad about her not being happy to see him? Maybe it was just too soon to expect so much.

"Where are you taking me? I'm going to Dad's office."

"I'll take you there," Arman replied softly. He didn't add '*eventually*' because he knew she wouldn't appreciate being led.

He was staring at her almost as if starving for a look from her. His eyes were trying to note each and every feature of hers. He noticed she wore a black French dress and it suited her. Her figure, when compared to the women he had dated, was somehow more appealing because he would not have to shower false praise which he was forced to give at times. Ria had everything that would make her an asset in his life. Physically she was an eyeful and mentally she was strong.

Now all he wanted to do was cup each and every part of her and kiss them. The taut way she was seated beside him didn't give him any room for even a hug. He wanted to tell her how much he missed talking to her but held his lips tight, looking straight ahead on the road as if his life depended on it.

"How have you been?" Ria asked after what she thought was a long, uncomfortable silence.

"It's been a long month," he answered and this time he looked at her again to meet her eyes.

Ria caught her breath. He looked tormented about it, but maybe she was imagining it!

"I'm here just to make Dad happy," she said, trying to change the topic. "He has sent me to collect some important files. He does not trust the courier."

"He should have told me then…"

"You would have come back to India then?"

They stopped at the traffic lights and Arman glanced at her with a frown, "If it was important enough, then yes, I would have Ria." His frown intensified, "What's wrong Ria? Your tone is all accusing. Have I done something wrong?"

"Oh…do I sound accusing? My so-called fiancé has been gone for a month; he doesn't feel the need to contact me even once and who I am to complain about it?" she said tauntingly, giving a grin which was far from encouraging. "No, I shouldn't complain! And I'm sorry for complaining…"

Arman pressed abruptly on the brakes in his car, almost hitting the cars in the front, in the process. Biting back a curse, he cast Ria an angry glance, "If you cared so much about talking to me, then why didn't you pick up the phone and call me? You had my number."

"Yeah, right!" she said, looking out and biting hard at her lower lip. "I didn't miss you enough to call you."

"Then *you* better stop complaining because I didn't miss you either."

That *hurt*. And badly too!

She tried not to feel anything though. Why should it matter that he didn't miss her? Well, he could go to hell for all she cared!

The rest of their drive was completed in a suffocating silence which neither of them was willing to break. So, as soon as the car halted, Ria scrambled out, and Arman rushed to do the same. But she didn't know where he had brought her as she looked at the tall glass building with awe.

"This isn't Dad's office...," she said slowly.

"That's right. It isn't," Arman locked the door of his BMW. "It's mine."

If she thought her father was rich, then she shouldn't have underestimated Arman's background. It was then that she realised what Arman must be dealing with every day. She silently acknowledged the slight twinge of respect that sprung up much against her wishes.

"This is where you work? It's a beautiful building," her voice came out a little hoarsely because of the tears she had tried to control.

Arman glanced at her, surprised at the compliment. Maybe she wanted to make another sarcastic reply!

"Thank you," he replied tersely. "It's been here for a while now. It's the fruit of all our brains," he said, walking around the entrance. "If you would come with me, I'll show you my office."

Ria looked at him and realised that all the excitement that Arman had displayed at the airport was missing. The man walking beside her was highly strung, she judged.

So he was angry.

She followed him timidly with all the signs of anger dissipating. Maybe for now she shouldn't comment on anything. All they needed was to have a candid talk without tearing at each other. Her eyes caught each and every graceful movement of his lithe body which moved swiftly with no-nonsense strides. The unleashed aura of command oozing out of him made her knees go weak. His hair was as always tied at the back of his head and once again she felt like touching them. He wore black trousers with a light blue printed shirt to go with it. The shirt sleeves were rolled back, as if his hands had been busy working before he had come to pick her up. Although she had never given much thought on how men dressed, Arman was certainly an exception. She noticed those suspenders lying across his shoulders to reach his waist, making him look incredibly sexy. When did suspenders make anyone look sexy? She was way too into him, she thought. If only he was in love with her…

She knew she had tested his patience far enough and he could snap any moment at her. But he had given her a tough time as well.

"You can come in," Arman said, standing at the entrance of his office and staring oddly at her.

Ria realised that she had followed him up till the sixth floor and hadn't even noticed it.

The glass doors opened and they entered a huge, spacious cabin. The wallpaper was done in black and white graphic design, giving way to the shape of a car. His desk and chair were placed at the centre of the room and his drawing-board took most of the space. She could smell the clean dark wood of mahogany inside and it felt cosy. It was really a nice place to work in. On the other side were two computers that were switched on, showing slide shows of the designs he must have been working on.

"How long does it take to design a car?"

Arman looked up from his laptop for a moment, ignoring the important e-mail he had been looking at. "Hmm, usually these are spur-of-the-moment designs. Everybody in the team comes up with his own ideas after which we tend to improvise. The best one gets a raise," he grinned when saying that.

"So it's not only you who works?"

"Well, I do know what kind of a design I want, so I make a sketch first," he smiled suddenly. "I own the company but I cannot handle things without my staff. They are an important part of what we are today," he said, turning back to the screen and wondering why Ria was so interested in him all of a sudden.

"You always wanted to design cars then?" Ria asked, fiddling with the chair and hoping she hadn't annoyed him with all her questions.

He smiled again, "All I knew was that I wanted to draw cars as it seemed more manly...," he laughed when she screwed her face, trying to understand what he was telling her. "I'm kidding! I don't want you to label me as a chauvinist."

She turned red at the implication and he realised then that his shot had hit the mark.

"We have some very talented people working with us; perhaps you would like to meet them?" he asked, sounding extra patient and even loving.

It was difficult to digest this new Arman.

"I want to become a teacher," she blurted without any excuse.

Arman closed his e-mail and looked up, "And?"

"I was thinking about doing postgraduation in education," she said, wondering a moment later why she was telling him all this! He must be least interested in her life.

"You will be a good teacher," his heart began to beat excitedly as he thought about the things he would like to teach her. She looked so innocent standing there, fiddling with things so as to hide her nervousness from him, but it was apparent she was.

She looked up and their eyes met. Something like a peace treaty passed between them and they smiled at each other.

"This is a very nice office," she said, trying to be as calm as possible. She even managed to maintain her smile.

"Be careful Ria or else I'll think that you like me."

Throwing him a haughty look, Ria didn't answer but turned away to look out of the window. Let him think what he wanted to.

"You can tell me if you don't like me," Arman ventured, trying to curb his frustration and desperately wanting her to feel the same way as he did about her.

"If you know it, then why ask me?" she queried rudely.

"If I know…!" Arman stared at her, shaking his head in disbelief. "Are we going to continue with this verbal battle so long as you stay here?"

Ria narrowed her eyes, "I won't be with you all the time, so you don't have to worry."

"You minx!" Arman took long strides to reach her and hold her tightly against him. "Why do you trouble me so much?"

Staring into his grey eyes, Ria swallowed hard. It was a

while since she had been so close to him. It did something to her. She had missed him so much, she realised then. Every moment had been impossible without him…

Earlier Arman had no intention of touching her, but holding her and feeling her softness against him just made him lose all his self-control.

She raised her lips to him, her eyes staring like two huge pools of fire. He felt a wild pleasure at just holding her next to him. No, he should not be doing that; it was not correct to use her like that.

"You didn't answer my question," he said, clearing his throat. His fingers tightened around her waist and his fingers dug into her soft flesh. He could feel the heat of her body even through her clothes.

"I…forgot the question," she said a little meekly.

Eyeing her minutely, Arman asked again, "Why do you trouble me so much? Why is it that whenever we talk, we land in a verbal battle?" he asked, unable to resist the urge to brush his lips against her forehead. As he gave in to his feelings, his eyes closed automatically to savour the moment of ecstasy while trying to control the shudders passing through his body. "I hate it when you do that."

"You…," Ria's hands came around him and she purred softly, "do what?"

"Ria…don't do this."

Arman suddenly became still and pulled his hands away. His face looked drawn and agitated. He dug his hands into his pockets and Ria couldn't help noticing the play of muscles around his shoulders. Gosh, she had even seen him naked…and she wanted to see it again.

"I'm sorry," she admitted at last. "I don't know what happens to me when I'm with you."

She was being honest and Arman felt the stirrings of hunger again. But nothing on his face showed what he was feeling inside. "You don't have to be sorry," he tried to acquit her from any guilt. "We are engaged now and it's normal for us to be attracted to each other."

Was that all, she thought dismally.

"Thank God you didn't say that because you are a man and I am a woman, it's *normal* for us to be attracted to each other."

"I'm not attracted to all women."

"Well that's a relief...," Ria said, her words laced with sarcasm. The smile was immediately wiped off from Arman's face.

Turning his back on her, Arman shook his head, "We are back to our verbal battle again, aren't we?"

"I don't want to fight with you," Ria said, pouting her lips.

"Thank God...now, why don't you sit down? I had a talk with your Dad and I have the file that he wants."

"Oh, so Dad told you I was coming," Ria said, her anger rising again. "Why can't he leave me alone?"

"Maybe you should empathise with him, Ria," he advised. As she opened her mouth to argue, he raised his hand, "I'll tell him not to worry about you any more. Will that make you happy?"

"That *might* relieve him since he must have taken for granted that you would be assuming my responsibility, no matter how much you despised it. You can never be too sure with Dad."

Shrugging his shoulders, Arman pressed the button on the intercom, "Send the file with Melhera Industries designs." As an afterthought, he added, "And two cups of coffee." Then looking at a perturbed Ria, he changed his mind, "Or rather, get us two Cokes with lots of ice."

"Right, sir."

Just when Ria thought their discussion was over, the knock on Arman's door made her turn to look at the intruder. She thought of the word 'intruder' because after missing him so much, she wanted to be alone with him. Wonder of wonders!

"You wanted Melhera Industries files, sir?"

Arman tipped his specs and nodded, "Yes, this is the one. Thank you, Mike."

When Arman looked at Ria to introduce them, he noticed the colour drain out of her face. She was blinking in shock. He jerked his eyes at Mike and his jaw tightened when he saw the betraying colour creep up into Mike's cheeks.

Did they know each other?

11

"Mike…"

Arman cleared his throat and took his specs off, cleaning the lens as if nothing was unusual about him. He eyed them silently for what it felt like more than an eternity. From the looks of it, he guessed they had met before.

He hadn't meant to ask but he couldn't stop himself, "You know him?"

Ria's eyes opened wide before moving towards Arman, "I'll be leaving soon."

Arman saw how scared she looked and trapped too. Maybe he should have a talk with her later. After all, Mike didn't have to know what kind of a relationship they shared; or maybe, he should.

"This is my fiancée, Mike."

Mike was the youngest executive in Arman's office. He was about twenty-four-years old, blond and white skinned.

With his smooth talks and good looks, he had reached this far. Despite everything else, he was hard working and Arman hadn't taken much notice of it so far till that day. He thought with irritation how it never crossed his mind that it could have been Mike of *all* the people!

"Congratulations then, sir," said Mike, looking as though he had swallowed an apple without biting it.

"You can leave now," Arman grimaced.

Ria stared at Mike and watched him until he had left the room. Arman turned his attention to her and noticed how pale she had become.

"Are you going to faint?"

"Do I have a choice?" she asked with a weak attempt at humour.

Arman frowned. If she wanted to escape the questions, then she would have said it right on his face.

"You know him, right?"

Ria fidgeted with her engagement ring and didn't look up before replying, "Yes I do."

"Don't think I'm interfering," he continued smoothly, "but as soon as Mike came in, you looked like you had seen a ghost…"

"Hmm…," she hedged, "I was just surprised to see him."

"Surprised?" he murmured the word softly. Taking off his glasses, he narrowed his eyes, "And why were you surprised?"

"Arman, do we have to discuss this?"

'Yes, we have to!' he wanted to scream but all he could do was to act indifferent. Was it not absolute rubbish that he really cared? If only she hadn't reacted the way she did and ignored Mike, then whatever had been their relationship, it would not have mattered. He wished he could forget the look on Ria's face, but he just couldn't.

What was Mike to her?

The temptation to pick up the phone and call Mike back was great, but all he did was to stare at Ria, trying to fathom her. And all she did was to stand in front of him, digging her nails in the insides of her palm and fidgeting with her engagement ring. It was a ring that Mr Melhera had handed him at their engagement ceremony when he was not sure of going through it all. And now that they were engaged, he couldn't help but wonder what it would have been like had he met her before!

"Stop staring at me in that way...," her voice turned a little hoarse.

"I'm not staring at you. I was expecting an answer," he said, shrugging his shoulders carelessly. He put on his specs and remarked, "Fine...I'm not interested in your past life, Ria. As far as I know, you are engaged to me right now," his gaze became fixed, "and we are going to stay that way."

Ria could hardly hear what he was saying as her mind was still reeling under the impact of seeing Mike face to face. And except for being surprised, he showed no other reaction. Maybe it didn't matter to him; maybe she didn't matter to him any more. Anyway, loving a married man was not on her agenda.

"Ria...," she heard Arman's voice from far off.

She looked at him with glazed eyes, "What...I would like to go home now Arman," she said, a tired smile curving around her pouty lips. "It's been a long flight..."

"Fine," his voice was far from polite now. "I'll send the

chauffeur with you and you can go and rest." Slumping down in his chair and threading his fingers together, he asked suddenly, "Will you have dinner with me tonight?"

"Huh…yeah, sure." Anything to get out of here, she thought miserably.

* * * * *

To meet Mike here of all the places and he hadn't changed a bit! He still looked good except that she no longer felt anything but distaste.

It hadn't been smooth sailing but then did relationships ever were? They had broken up four months ago and she had been sourly tempted to kill him when she discovered his marital status. Instead she felt relieved that she had escaped from an embarrassing situation and all that she wanted was to forget him. Such people were not worth remembering anyway!

What had shocked her nonetheless was how innocent Mike looked. How could he still manage to look thus? Hate was a word she could never associate with him. All she could feel was hurt and betrayal. How Mike had withdrawn from her as soon as she had broken up, as if he had been waiting to get rid of her. It hadn't bothered her much then but within her heart of hearts, she had felt the urge to get back at him. But what could she have said to a man like Mike – that he didn't deserve to live? Maybe he didn't!

Oh! How she hated men!

On reaching home, she barely managed to take her clothes off. However, she was relieved to find her room cosy and her bed decent enough to fall into. She immediately fell asleep which indeed was a relief as so much was going on in her mind. As she drifted into a long restless sleep, she thought about Arman and how a marriage had been forced upon her, when all she wanted to do was run away.

* * * * *

Arman had expected her to be a punctual girl, but when he arrived at her house and she did not emerge from her room, his patience ran out. It was surprisingly a beautiful, three-storeyed mansion, devoid of unnecessary decorations. His own apartment was completely different to this one and he longed to take her to his apartment and show her around. She would like it; maybe she would come to love it…

Sighing, he realised how foolish his thoughts were and the way Ria had reacted on seeing Mike, he decided there was no chance of her falling in love with him. And he couldn't expect it either. After all, what woman would have liked to put up with the torture of living under one roof without love? Moreover, Ria had a mind of her own and was not susceptible to emotional blackmail.

Maybe he should have courted her just as any guy would have on meeting a girl for the first time.

Ringing the doorbell wasn't helping either. So he did what most desperate men would have done. He barged in.

The look of the house from outside was modest but he had underestimated the interiors. Inside, it was simply lavish and beautiful. Amitab Melhera had good taste, he thought. If only he had come earlier and met Ria, instead of just imposing himself on her. He should have acted like a sane man.

After all, he had only verbally consented to marry Amitab Melhera's daughter. He was on the pleasing mode at that time of his life. Nevertheless, it was a totally illogical explanation, even to him. It would have been so simple if he had kept in touch with his so-called fiancée, he thought quietly.

As he climbed up the stairs, he paused for a second as if he should have called out to her by her name...after all, that would be the right thing to have done, instead of intruding on her privacy.

"Ria...," he called out softly. Then a little loudly, "*Ria*!"

No one was at home; that was an odd thing. Didn't Amitab Melhera take care of his daughter in a foreign land? Shouldn't he have kept a housekeeper at least? Maybe he should have had a talk with Ria's father. He could have always given the excuse that he was only considering the safety of his fiancée after all. He suddenly felt concerned that it was not safe to really trust the housekeepers when the crime rate was going up. Maybe he should have volunteered himself...

He heard a loud scream and his heartbeat stopped for a minute second. All random thoughts disappeared as panic settled in.

Ria!

He ran in the direction of the scream and tore open the door of the room, where he guessed Ria was. He wished to God that she was there...

And there she was, lying unconcerned on her bed, the bedcovers thrown all over the place. He was certain that her clothes must have been strewn around among those, because when she twisted around the bed, he noticed her in her bare essentials. That was fine with him as he had seen a woman naked; another one wouldn't have bothered him. After all, this was her house, her room and she had the right to be comfortable as she was.

If only he could curb his restrained desire. Calming his nerves, he went in further and noticed her moving around. She was no longer screaming but he could see that her sleep had been troubled. He leaned down and touched her shoulder with the tip of his fingers, almost scared that he would jump right into the bed with her.

Damn it Arman, control yourself...

Ria jerked away from his touch and he pulled his hand away as if having touched a searing flame.

"Ria..." he said softly, pulling her hair away from her face. Her long curly hair looked beautiful when left open. Why did she keep them tied always? He really loved it when it flowed around her face.

"Hmmm...," she murmured and opened her eyes. At first her lips curved into a smile, but when she registered that it was him hovering worriedly around her, she let out another scream.

"What's wrong?" she heard him say anxiously. "And I thought we were going out for dinner."

"A...Arman...," she tried to get up, almost forgetting that she was wearing only a pair of white panties and bra. As she raised herself, she gasped as she felt his eyes move helplessly on the round moulds of her breasts. The tips of her nipples hardened involuntarily. With half open eyes, she grabbed the blanket and met his eyes. He looked handsome as always. She sighed deeply, hating the way her body responded to him.

"Why...," she saw him swallow before saying, "why don't you dress up while I wait for you outside?"

"Huh?"

His eyes lingered a little longer than they should have, but he forcibly tore his eyes away from her breasts. Suddenly she felt like giggling but bit the insides of her cheeks instead. She pulled the sheet up and nodded, "Okay."

When Ria came out, all she wore was blue jeans and a white T-shirt. Her hair was tied into a tight bun on the top of her head in a messy manner. Arman frowned and blinked at her. Was she the same woman he had seen naked in the bed?

Well, *almost* naked...

"I thought I would take you out to a classy restaurant...," he began.

"I don't want to go out," she told him and her words were final. "I'm tired. I don't think I can even move a muscle."

He opened his mouth to say something, but she raised her eyes and gave him a strange look. He suddenly felt amused...and very much in love.

"Then I'll go," he said politely and took out his specs from his pockets and put them on. "You can rest."

He walked back to the door with a heavy heart, wishing he could spend the evening with her. Maybe it was for the good because one more minute in her company might have made him take leave of his senses.

"Uh Arman...," he heard her voice, coming out hesitantly for a change.

Turning, he looked enquiringly towards her, "Yes?"

"Would you like to stay for dinner?"

Arman couldn't remember the last time when he had spent time with a woman like that. Though given an alternative, he would have loved to ravish her and he remembered never getting to spend time with Ria. They had always been fighting and arguing, but then it was different. She looked so pretty sitting there by the stove, chopping vegetables and she did look like she could cook. What exactly did he know about her?

"You are looking strangely at me," she commented, her eyes darting straight to meet his.

"I was wondering what if you could cook!" he lied swiftly.

Her eyes didn't leave his, "It's just vegetable stew and bread."

"Not an Indian dish?"

Ria had the grace to blush, "I…don't know much about Indian cuisine. I'll learn it though."

Arman raised his brows, "You are not trying to sell yourself on it, are you?"

"I'm not selling myself for anything," she snapped and turned her eyes to the simmering pot.

"Ria…I didn't mean that," he said quietly, loosening his tie with a sigh. "And you know it."

They were quiet for some time as Arman went about, laying the table without being asked. For several minutes they worked harmoniously and Ria seemed peaceful throughout. Glancing at Arman, Ria felt the desire for something. Was he going to touch her tonight? She wished he would, as she poured herself the first helping of the stew.

"How do you know Mike?" the words seemed be forced out from his lips with his eyes showing visible distress.

Ria forgot to breathe for a second, "Huh?"

"Ria…," Arman cocked his head, "I know you heard me."

Frowning, Ria took in a deep breath and said, "He is the same guy I spoke about earlier."

"The married man?"

"Hmm…"

The stew was made very well but to Arman it tasted like ash. This was the same guy Ria loved so much? The guy who was right in his office? Blood boiled in his head and anger surged through his body as he tried to control himself by looking disinterested.

"For how long…," he started to ask but the look in her eyes made him stop.

"What Mike and I had was a complete sham, Arman and I really don't like remembering that part of my life."

Arman wanted to argue but maybe it wasn't the right moment. He leaned back and folded his arms defensively, "See, you reacted so strongly." He added defensively, "I can't ignore it and you keep on prolonging the torture by keeping me in suspense!"

"Arman…," she didn't know what to say.

"Fine, if that is what you want. I won't raise this topic again but don't expect me to forget it either." He looked angry but then why was he? "I think I should leave."

"Without having your dinner?"

Arman shrugged, "I don't have a taste for it any more…"

"Then the door is that way," Ria muttered, trying not to give way to tears.

Arman gaped at her, wanting to say much but leaving it all unsaid. Instead he asked, "Did you miss me, Ria?"

The question surprised her and she replied carelessly, "We don't have a relationship that has any room for such sentiments, Arman…"

Her words cut him through and suddenly he felt vulnerable. No, it wouldn't do. Feeling the way he did was like giving her a whole lot of power over him. Maybe he should just leave; so he did just that. He didn't wait for her to complete what she had to say.

"Arman…," he heard his name being called but he kept on walking.

Ria stared perplexed. Why didn't he wait for some more time and listen to what she had to say? Usually he never got annoyed when she spoke angrily. Didn't he laugh it off or answer her back when they got into arguments? What had changed?

Frowning, she concluded that maybe he was fed up with her and didn't want to waste time in arguing with her. Now she was pretty sure he didn't even like her. Maybe he was spending a night with Christina, who seemed much livelier a companion than her. The thought made her fingers itch to throw something…so she threw the remaining contents of the stew into the bin.

That night Ria couldn't sleep. She did not expect to anyway as it had been the most stressful day of her life.

Meeting Mike, Arman behaving oddly and…

The sudden knock on the door startled her. Scrambling out of her bed, Ria hurried downstairs. Who could have come at that hour? Hoping against hopes that it was Arman, Ria opened the door with an excited smile…

"*Mike*!" her voice came out in a squeak.

She didn't get the chance to say more. He rushed in, sweeping her into his arms and kissing her ardently. His lips ran expertly over hers as if he had never forgotten the feel of them. Ria thought she was dreaming but the moment she opened her mouth to protest, she felt him invade her mouth with his tongue.

"Oh…Ria, I missed you so much! Why did you have to go?"

"If only you would let me *breathe*!" she snapped and pushed him away, rubbing her lips with the back of her hand. "What was that for?"

"I thought about us a lot…"

"Thought about us, my foot!" Ria almost screamed. "I don't want to even look at your face, Mike. Just get the hell out of my house."

Mike's face changed expressions rapidly as he had never expected Ria to protest. "I love you!"

The words, which would have meant something to her a few months ago, scratched in her ears like an irritant. In fact, she found him a pain and wanted to be rid of him. But all she did was to glower at him with dark, expressionless eyes. "I said get out of my house Mike. You are one of those who do not understand when told something. Go back to your wife!"

He took a step forward as if going to grab her again, but

suddenly stopped on seeing her clench her teeth with resentment.

"I thought you still cared..."

"I care a...," she muttered the word to herself and moved away. "Thanks for coming here and making a fool of yourself..."

"I can't help it if my wife came to know about us...," he sulked. "Everything was going just fine!"

Ria turned red at his words, realising what place she had been given in his life. And to think that she had loved him! She wanted to curl up and die of shame but that could happen later. At that moment, her uppermost thought was to get him out of her sight. "If you have said enough, I would like you to leave," she said, her anger giving way to indifference. "You don't care about me, Mike. It was just a passing affair..."

"But..."

"Just go," she rubbed her forehead, closing her eyes in pain. "Go!"

He hesitated for a second before turning to leave, his shoulders slumped in defeat.

"I hate you! And I hate myself!" she yelled as she heard the sound of his car leaving her doorway.

Then she broke down, crying in pathetic sobs.

The next day when Arman was expecting Ria to sulk at home because of his abrupt departure, he saw her enter his office. She was wearing a simple A-line cut denim blue skirt with a baby pink tank top, her hair tied as always. She looked haunted and her eyes were swollen. Was it something he had done?

She entered his room without knocking and he didn't mind. The previous night he had behaved badly and Ria had been playing on his mind!

"I wasn't expecting you at the office," he stated, sitting quietly behind his desk and staring at her intently.

"I wasn't expecting to come to your office either," she said with a sigh. "I just wanted to tell you I'm leaving and going back to India."

Her words caught him by surprise, "I thought you loved it here…"

"I thought so too," her eyes turned nostalgic and Arman smiled to himself.

"Sit down…"

She hesitated at the door but then came in, looking visibly tense.

Arman jumped out of his chair and his eyes glittered dangerously, never leaving the sight of her lips. They looked red and bitten…

"Do you have bugs in your house?" he asked, each word getting dragged out of his mouth.

"*What*? Why?" she looked confused.

"Your lips Ria…"

Her fingers immediately went and touched them. She looked up to find him looking furious and for a moment she felt a little scared. Should she tell him?

"It was a bug," she muttered.

At least that's what Mike was!

"Let me have a look."

"No!" Ria swallowed hard. "I…I'll be fine."

Arman purposefully got up from his chair, his eyes never

leaving her lips and daring her to move. He sat down on the desk in front of her and leaning down, pulled her fingers away before touching her lips nonchalantly. It felt as it had felt when he had touched her lips earlier…malleable and sensuous. But his eyes showed none of his feelings except for fury.

"This doesn't look like a bug bite," his words came out in a whisper.

Ria turned away from his probing gaze and felt a palpitating tension in the room. She wanted to look at Arman but couldn't meet his eyes.

"Who was he?"

Ria replied in a small voice, "I told you it was a bug…"

Arman's hands came and rested roughly on the sides of her chair and his mouth turned pale around its corners. "Do you think I'm naïve enough to believe that?"

She couldn't meet his eyes then. Deliberately pulling up her face with his thumb and forefinger, he met her gaze squarely, "Look at me Ria, for God's sake! You look hurt…"

"I don't want to talk about it," she blazed, placing her fingers on his in a bid to escape from his hold. "And let me go!"

"Ria…," Arman said without letting go of his hold, "you were bitten on your lip, damn it!"

"It wasn't supposed to be…," Ria sucked in a breath when she saw how her words affected him.

"Someone kissed you," he stated flatly. He took his hands away, but Ria didn't make any bid to escape. What was wrong with him? He was sounding as if he was hurt inside!

But he looked as impassive as a mime. It bothered her that he could read her so well.

"He took me by surprise, Arman and I didn't know…"

"I'll kill him!" he got down from the desk, walking right out of his office. Ria came running behind him, dragging him in by his arm.

"Arman, don't make a scene. Please."

"I'm not kidding, Ria. I…"

"First come inside," she begged, her heart beating fast. She all but hauled him inside his office and closed the door with a firm click. As soon as she turned, Arman pulled her into his arms, burying his face in the crook of her neck. The shock of his nearness was so poignant that Ria felt her eyes prick with tears. But this time it wasn't because she was sad; she felt deliriously happy. It was at that moment that she realised, maybe…maybe she did feel something more than hate for Arman.

"Arman…," she whispered. "What happened?"

"I don't know," he murmured like a little kid needing assurance. She curled her palm at his back and stayed there.

"I'm fine Arman…I really am."

"You are hurt," he whispered.

"Hmm…but it doesn't hurt. It will go away."

He rubbed his nose, his nostrils tingling with her scent. She smelled an odd combination of roses and jasmine. He wanted to say more but his heart felt constricted.

"Ria, I…"

"Arman don't worry about me," Ria said, her fingers caressing and feeling his muscles react. "Arman…"

"Oh God...," he moved his face from her neck as his lips unerringly probed hers, touching them softly. He said against them, "I don't like it if anyone hurts you...every part of you is precious to me."

Ria's breath came out in small uneven breaths. What was in this man that affected her so much? Even Mike didn't make her respond that way. With Arman, she wanted to just give in. But that's what she was scared of...

Of giving in...

"Arman...just...," Ria tried to push him away as the memories of the previous night came to plague her mind.

Mike's brutal kiss, Mike's harsh words...

She hated him.

She hated men!

"Ria, why didn't you tell me?"

Uncertain of herself and Arman, Ria couldn't answer. Why didn't she tell him?

"I was scared."

It was a relief when he didn't probe further. She really wouldn't have known how to answer him. Even though Arman's arms gave her a lot of comfort, she couldn't say that she didn't want to run away again.

"I have to go," were the next words that came out of her lips, her throat tightening with discomfort. She didn't want to cry again. She never wanted to cry for something she didn't think worthy of it and Mike was definitely not worth any more of her tears. After all, was that a reason enough to cry? So many people had boyfriends who betrayed them...

"Arman...just leave me!"

And he did. There was a peculiar look on his face. She wouldn't have worried if Arman had got angry, but she saw him look tortured again.

"When do you want to leave?"

"Right now."

"Fine." He turned away, deliberately not facing her. Tears streamed down her cheeks as she moved towards the exit. Was there anything else to talk about?

"Ria," his voice came out quietly, "if you are thinking about breaking off the engagement, then forget about it. I'm still going to marry you and I'm going to do it fast..."

Ria eyes widened with each word, "Fa...fast?"

"I'm going to India with you," he said firmly, meeting her eyes. His grey eyes revealed next to nothing when he announced, "And then you are going to be my wife."

12

By the time they reached Delhi, Ria was fuming with anger and disappointment. Arman showed no reaction. He was calm and cool all through their journey, working calmly on his laptop or closing his eyes to sleep. She looked into the small screen attached to the seat in front of her, watching him stealthily. He didn't once look at her with interest. It was as if he had switched off the button of reactions within. It shouldn't have bothered her though. He was a brute and would always be and he was true to his word.

They were getting married at last. Her father hadn't bothered to question Arman (sometimes she felt he knew all along that it would happen) and her mother was a conspirator in it all. It was as if she was viewing her life being written out for her. Very few people were invited and she really didn't care. Guests or no guests, Arman would marry her. He went ahead and helped her Dad arrange everything.

The problem was that though she felt like retaliating, she didn't exactly feel wretched. She didn't understand her own feelings…that put her in a dilemma as she could not decide whether to confront Arman or not. He wouldn't listen to her anyway. Why bother!

"If only you could stop moping…," her mother said, "you would make a beautiful bride."

"That's what I'm trying to say. Arman is too good-looking for me. Why did you have to find *him* of all the men!"

"Not again, Ria."

With a sigh, Vidhya gave the last finishing touches to her makeup and said, "I will wait for you outside. If you are finished, your Dad wants to talk to you."

"Do you think anyone would notice if I was missing?"

Vidhya's lips twisted into an ironic smile, "I think we would, so you better get ready."

"I hate this!" Ria grumbled as she glared at herself in the mirror, "and I hate the high-handedness of all the men. They just want a woman who would say 'yes' to everything they say…I hate men," she continued as she fiddled with her hair, messing up the sophisticated hairstyle, "and I hate…"

"You are going to get married now, so you better stop cribbing," her father's irritated voice interrupted. "And you look good enough. Come out."

"What's with you? I'm ready. Tell your lover boy to…," she saw the play of conflicting emotions on her father's face and stopped abruptly, "I'm ready."

Amitab Melhera sighed deeply, "You are going to face a lot of trouble if you continue with this kind of attitude, Ria. I thought you both had begun to get along by now."

"I don't care."

Amitab gave a sad chuckle, "That's what I was afraid of."

The wedding was quiet and a quick one. Amitab Melhera didn't like it one bit as his only daughter was getting married. Surely it called for a celebration and it was not something to be embarrassed about. What was strange was that they were entering into an arranged marriage in which neither the groom nor the bride was interested. However, on looking at Arman's placid face, no one could have said that he was being forced into a marriage. If only he had showed some reaction!

He waited for Ria to step out of her room and when she did, he showed not even a flicker of interest and nor did his face reveal that he was marrying her out of pity. However, Ria was a tough nut to crack. She looked at Arman as if it was a burden for her to just exist on the planet. Ria's Dad noticed that if she didn't stop behaving the way she was doing, Arman was bound to lose his patience.

They went around the scared pyre as the *pandit* recited the *shlokas* which sounded like hollow words to her. Amitab thought marriage actually meant that the two persons would be planning a life together. He himself had chosen Vidhya because he had loved her…

Before he could think about anything else, the marriage ceremony came to an end. Finally Arman and Ria were married and Amitab let out a sigh of relief. He however felt depressed that he would have to live with the guilt all his life that Arman and Ria didn't love each other…how was he going to bear that?

How could Ria bear that, she didn't know.

Arman was nowhere to be seen. They were supposed to be spending their wedding night in her room. It was decorated beautifully. There were flowers everywhere – pink and red rose petals were strewn on her bed and the carpet spread in a way that invited her to just slip in without any excuse. In fact she didn't want to make any excuses that night.

She glanced at the huge wall clock on her wall. It was nearly midnight and she had been waiting for two hours now. Maybe he didn't want to sleep with her. The knowledge gave her a bitter feeling of unrest, which added to her sorrow and worry.

She didn't want to sleep with him either. All she wanted to do was to be left alone. Alone…alone… alone…she closed her eyes to stop the tears from rolling down. All she knew was that she was slipping slowly into subconsciousness where she didn't feel anything but loneliness. Soon she was fast asleep.

Late into the night, when she felt another body sink into the space beside her, all she did was to mumble something. She didn't say anything when that someone took her clothes off one by one. Strong hands followed the shape of her crevice, cupping the plump ends, holding them and squeezing them softly while making her purr under her breath. His hands no longer caressed, but became still and uncertain all of a sudden.

She smiled when she heard a hiss of controlled breath beside her as if caught in a frozen silence.

"Ria…," she felt Arman's hands shake her lightly.

"Arman…," she murmured softly, relishing and rolling his name on her tongue. "Hmm…"

Arman shook her again, filling his eyes with her glorious body. He breathed in to keep himself in control.

"Are you awake?"

She tried to but failed miserably, "Do I have to?"

"If you don't, then I will have to."

Ria rolled in the opposite direction to his and ducked her head under her pillow, her nostrils filling up with the fragrance of roses. She sniffed the perfume for a second and then dozed off again.

"Ria!" His voice came out so loudly that Ria sat up on the bed, naked and disoriented.

"Huh...what...*what's* wrong?" Her hair was tied and Arman leaned behind her and unclipped them. As they rolled down to her waist, he breathed a sigh of relief. "What's wrong with you? Wake up."

Ria still couldn't comprehend what he was saying; his hands felt good when he touched her hair, curling the ends around his fingers. His face was shadowed in the darkness but his breathing was far from normal. Hers didn't feel normal either.

She blinked, trying to look at Arman...and when she did, she stopped breathing. He looked like a Greek God on earth.

Wrong.

Greek god on her bed.

His hair was still tied and only his specs were off and by the look of it, he was naked.

"You look beautiful," he whispered as he leaned more and more, making her lie down on her back. She stared helplessly into his face, with his sharp eyes mirroring his emotions. His palms cupped her face, kissing her forehead lightly, "I feel like kissing you all over like this...," he punctuated his words with a kiss each. He kissed all over her face except on her lips. She leaned back, digging her head into the soft pillow and trying to resist herself, but failing. She didn't feel like resisting...

"Arman..."

"Beautiful hair...," he moved his hands down, his hands barely touching her hard-tipped breasts and trembling navel. He took hold of her hands and brought them forcibly around his neck. "Don't be scared sweet..." When she tried to pull back, he uttered, "I just want..."

"Want me?" she completed for him, her throat dry with anticipation and a little fear.

"Yes...I want you...I wanted you for my wife, Ria for so long!" he groaned when her hands tightened around his neck. He brought his lips down and touched them lightly with hers, breathed in to inhale her scent...loving the feel of her skin all the while.

"For a long time?"

"At least since the day I saw you...," he voiced honestly, his hips shifting over hers. He rolled on his back, taking her with him and making her gasp loudly. The feel was so arousing that she could feel the cleft of her core throb visibly. She hardly heard his words as she melted into him. "Since the day I touched you, I have wanted you...although your sharp tongue somehow had a negative effect on me."

"Was...was that a good thing?"

"It's your tongue that keeps me around all the time... and your body...you are so lush...so full...," he groaned, "*I love...*"

Her ears perked at the words and she held her breath, "You love…what?"

"Kiss me," he said pulling her closer and she did, just a small little peck that made him chuckle. "Do all virgins act like you do?"

"Maybe," she answered absent-mindedly. "Arman, you were saying…"

"Why do you talk so much…," he parted her legs and Ria moved it on the either side of his hips, "Oh…yes…that's good."

Giving in, Ria laughed as his movements impatiently, when hers were automatic. She wanted him too…just as much as he did. Maybe it wouldn't be so bad making love to him.

Making love to him…

"Arman!" she shouted when she couldn't take his teasing any more, "Take me…*ahhh*…!"

"Now?" his voice resounded in her ears.

"*Now,*" she barely managed to nod.

He rolled back again, looming on her, crushing her breasts in his hands and relishing the feel of them. He wanted to sink in her and forget the world. He wanted to make her his forever…and convey how he felt about her; how deeply he felt about their marriage.

He would want her, love her…

He sunk in her just as easily as he would slip on mossy moorland. Although there was a certain tightness that stopped him but made him just want to go on and on…his heart beat fast…then faster…and she tightened more. His eyes closed as something dawned to him.

"Ria..."

"Don't stop..."

"I *can't*," he gritted, closing his eyes in pure agony, "I can't...stop...but..."

"Oh Arman...*harder*..."

"Oh God...!"

Her words did him in and he moved harder, deeper, holding her tightly because the ecstasy was taking too long to come and too soon to endure. They rolled on their backs, breathing in loudly. Then with a loud groan, Arman came. He came for long, as if emptying his soul into her but another void settled in when they quietened.

The ends of Ria's hair stuck on his chest and he plucked them off one by one, thoughtfully.

Ria opened her eyes after a minute, smiling into his eyes. Her eyes shone with what he had hoped for since their engagement, but they didn't mean anything to him right then. All he could remember was to feel himself enter her and there was no pain...nor was there any painful recuperation.

"Ria," his voice sounded hollow.

"Hmm?"

"You are not a virgin."

13

"Good guess," Ria replied as she pulled away from him, the glow of lovemaking fading from her face and disappearing in the tightness of her voice.

Arman's eyes looked accusing. In fact he didn't look like a man who had made love to his wife a few minutes ago. The way he had held her almost deceived her into believing that Arman felt more than just lust. She had felt his love, evidently from the way he touched her while coaxing her into his arms.

All of a sudden it felt like a dream now.

"You didn't tell me."

"I'm sleepy," she answered instead, turning her naked back to him, though the folds of her plump waist wanted him to pull her back into his arms.

"That wasn't the answer I was expecting...," he said sharply, dispelling all the warmth she was feeling for him.

"Not that it bothers me. I was just surprised."

"Thank you very much. I'm sure you are not a virgin either, so I don't think either of us should be bothered."

He opened his mouth to argue but closed it when her eyes started flaring.

"Are we going to fight again?"

"If you want to," she returned quickly.

"Go to sleep, Ria," Arman said in a tired voice. "I don't want to do anything with you right now."

"I don't want to do anything with you from now onwards!" she answered, anger flaring in her dark eyes as she hopped out of the bed. "You *hypocrite*! Just because I didn't come with a compact vagina, you think you have the right to look at me like that!"

Arman's lips tightened around the corners at her words, "I haven't said anything to you yet."

"As if you have to! Just look at yourself…," Ria lips trembled with barely controlled rage. "You wanted sex. Now that it's over, you remember that I don't have a..."

"Don't say the word," he warned her, his body tightening. "I never said a word about…"

"Fine, I won't say the word! Thanks for the night…I'll sleep somewhere else." She turned to leave when his arms came around her tightly, almost knocking the breath out of her. Her breasts got crushed under the impact and though it should have hurt her, all she could feel was desire.

"Leave me *alone*!" she yelled, denying the pleasure she felt for him.

She wanted to hate him, but damn her body…it was betraying her again.

"Not while you are my wife," he growled, flipping her easily on the bed.

Her eyes widened as he pinned her arms at the sides of her face, "What are you doing? I don't want you to touch me!"

"You let him touch you…why not me?"

"You bastard!"

His eyes flared, "Don't resort to name calling, sweetheart…it's our wedding night."

"You had your share of wedding night. Now you can leave me alone," she tried to fight his arms off frantically. "Damn it, Arman…let go *off me…*," she bit her lip when she felt him cover his body with hers. "*Now,* what are you doing?"

"Making you shut up. I don't want your parents to think I'm raping you."

The thought clicked and she closed her mouth abruptly, "They won't think that way." Her eyes searched his, "Will they?"

Her reaction took him completely off guard. He had expected her to yell more but all she did was look at him with those trusting eyes. Damn…damn…damn…

"Go off to sleep," he rolled off her, leaving her feeling cold and lonely once again. "We can discuss about your lack of compact vagina later."

"If you have to discuss it later, why not do it now?" she muttered.

Arman didn't have the courage to say more though he wondered why didn't she realise how it hurt to know that he wasn't the first man in her life? It almost broke his heart into pieces but he didn't say anything. All he did was to stare into the darkness, his thoughts turning bitter and unpleasant.

"The arranged marriage didn't do much for us, did it?" his voice carried a hollow note. "Neither you nor I wanted to go ahead with this marriage but now I regret that I didn't listen to you..."

"Why are you saying all this?" Ria was almost scared out of her wits. Arman sounded as if he had given up on her. Had he? Did her virginity matter to him that much? One mistake, one night and here she had to face her husband on her wedding night! Not that everything had turned out to be bad...she had never felt so desired or so cherished ever before in her life.

'Please don't give up!' she wanted to cry, but all she could do was to stare at him with numb senses. She however concluded that an angry Arman was safer than a despairing one.

"I mean I should have listened to you. I should have left you alone...," Arman turned his back to her. "I'm tired suddenly...are you?"

"N...no," Ria replied, reaching out and hesitantly touching his shoulder, "Arman, I wanted to tell you..."

Usually she avoided using his name but his name sounded good on her lips, just as he had in her arms. Maybe Arman realised it too because he jerked a little and took a long deep breath.

"Don't touch me." It was first time that he used those words and that hurt badly.

"Arman...listen to me...I..."

Arman turned again and his eyes glittered with barely

controlled anger. "What the hell do you want now? You cannot give me love; you cannot give yourself to me...I don't want a doll to hold...I want a real woman with real feelings."

"Oh really?" anger flared in her eyes too. "Do you think I'm not woman enough to offer you that?"

"I think you are selfish, Ria. I pity the man who must have satisfied your lust!"

Ria couldn't stop raising her hand and hitting him before he could even react. A sharp, painful silence ascended in the bedroom and for a heart-stopping moment, Arman sat frozen in his place. The next thing he did was to jump out of the bed, pull his pillow out and growl, "That's the last straw! You deserve this cold bed. I'm getting out of here!"

"You had no right to say that to me," she spluttered.

"Why didn't you tell me you were physically involved before?"

Ria blinked her eyes and pulled in a sharp breath, "I didn't get a chance Arman...and I thought there was nothing to tell. I hadn't been planning to get married."

"I almost feel betrayed." Arman felt he had said too much and could have bitten his tongue at his folly. What did Ria care if he felt betrayed? She wasn't in love with him now, was she? All she cared about was herself and how to get out of this loveless arrangement...

Now they were married.

"That day when your lip was bitten...did you both..."

Ria stopped breathing, "Please...I didn't sleep with Mike that night, Arman..."

Arman stared at for a brief moment, then sighed, "No, you couldn't have."

Tears welled in her eyes at his simple acceptance. He took a sharp breath, "I don't know why I keep assuming things about you."

"I'm sorry," she apologised without realising why she was doing so. Perhaps to quieten him; to convince him; to humour him!

"It doesn't matter now."

"Arman, don't do this..."

Arman walked out of her room without looking back. He was as naked as a new-born baby and not a wee bit self-conscious about his nudity. He was so beautiful...and she was not.

She wondered why he had felt betrayed when neither of them knew about their engagement. She, of course, never planned to enter into a permanent relationship. It had just happened – something which she regretted but never told anyone. She had never made any significant friends in her life, so it didn't matter at that time. In retrospect it did seem odd!

"Do you want to leave me?" Ria managed to spell out the words.

"I think it's what you want, so it's no use pretending otherwise..."

"*No!*"

He looked at her with eyes that could have killed a weak-hearted person, but Ria was built of stronger material. She knew he was not going to listen to her.

Walking out of her room had been the most difficult thing for him to do. It was his wedding night, yet it felt as a doomsday for him and he could have sworn that his heart hurt. Why did she behave that way? Why couldn't she just say outright what she had felt?

He couldn't find the answer to all his questions, but then, he couldn't force her to talk either. What she was hiding within would only hurt her in the end and that was something he couldn't bear, despite everything.

They didn't speak for two days; neither did they look at each other. Ria didn't say a word after the night they had spent together and Arman looked as impassive as ever. He didn't touch her any more. Not that she wanted him to; she defended herself as the nights turned gloomy and lonely. Without saying a word, Ria had taken her pillow and blanket and moved out of her room. The next morning she was surprised to find Arman missing from the room. Maybe he hadn't slept in her room either. Arman was deliberately trying to avoid her, Ria assumed. In fact he seemed to have become unduly busy with work.

If she thought they were successful in hiding the situation of their marriage, then she was thoroughly mistaken. Both Vidhya and Amitab were watching them closely.

'Enough is enough!' Ria wanted to say this, but she sat quietly in the corner of the sofa, tucking her legs in and flipping through a magazine that she was least interested in.

"I feel like hitting you Amitab," Vidhya whispered into her husband's ear. "And you know why?"

Amitab Melhera cleared his throat, "I'm keeping Arman busy with work…he has a contract to fulfil…"

"Damn you and your contract!" Vidhya pointed towards her daughter. "Does she look married to you in any manner?

I thought you got them married because that was what they wanted."

"Arman does like her, I know that," Amitab put in defensively. "It's not that I literally pushed them together..."

"Then Arman doesn't care now...and you are sleeping on the sofa tonight!" Vidhya spluttered as she walked away from a distressed husband to talk to her daughter.

Well, let him think what he wanted!

"Want to go shopping? I was thinking about a makeover" Vidhya asked in a cheerful voice.

Ria looked up with empty eyes, "Huh?"

Vidhya felt like crying but she did the opposite. At that moment what Ria needed was cheerfulness around and not tears, "What's wrong?"

"N...nothing Mom," Ria turned her eyes back to the magazine she was reading. "Nothing is wrong."

"Missing Arman?"

Ria just shook her head.

"Then why aren't you with him?"

"Mom...," Ria began in a dragging tone. "Arman and I aren't on good terms right now..."

"But you both are married!"

"Well, marriage doesn't change anything! If you thought sleeping together would change the fact, then you are absolutely wrong!"

"Ria!" Vidhya turned a little pale. "I didn't raise you to talk to me like that."

"Then don't talk to me about this, Mom."

"Yeah sure, you can talk about this to me," she heard Arman say. Ria jumped out of the sofa, delighted to catch a glimpse of him, but one look at his face warned her not to say a word further.

"Oh hi!" Vidhya got up self-consciously. "We were just talking about you..."

"So I could hear. Can I get a drink?"

"What?"

"You heard me sweetheart," Arman voiced almost viciously. "Get me something to drink."

"Will poison do?"

Vidhya retreated on the sofa again, her eyes wide with amazement. What was wrong with both of them?

"If you promise to share," Arman responded easily.

"Get it yourself then!" Ria yelled. Climbing out of the sofa, she headed straight for her bedroom.

Vidhya swallowed hard, carefully keeping her thoughts to herself. Maybe she should have a talk with her husband on this matter. Either way, she knew that she and Amitab could not solve this issue.

Arman followed suit and glared at his wife, "Can't you get your husband a glass of water? Do you want me to beg?"

"I'm your wife, not your slave. And I don't like threats," she answered stiffly.

"Damn it, Ria! You are so difficult...," he sat down suddenly, closing his eyes tightly and rubbing his temples hard. "You are a self-opinionated woman who hates even the sight of me..."

Ria felt tears trickle down her cheeks, "Arman..."

"I can't bear it...*God* save me!"

"Don't say that!" she wiped away her cheeks quickly. "I'm not selfish, I do care about you."

Arman lifted his head and stared at her hard, "Words, words, words...they don't satisfy..." Arman felt his head swim. He had been surviving on coffee for the past two days and the hot summer was something he wasn't used to yet. Sleep was something that eluded him. Maybe he should take a shower and sleep for some time, but he had to go and...

"Arman..."

Ria couldn't decipher what was happening to him. She saw his face turn abnormally pale as he kept shifting from one place to another. She took a step forward, sensing something was wrong. Arman didn't look like a person she had seen a few days ago. He wasn't wearing his glasses and his eyes seemed sunken with dark circles. His shirt sleeves were pulled over his arms and looked wrinkled. His hair was slicked back and he hadn't groomed himself as he always did.

Arman was suddenly sinking back in the bed, the corner of his mouth turning as grey as his eyes. "Ria...I..."

"*Oh...!*"

This time Ria ran towards him as he fell, but she wasn't strong enough to hold him upright. She kept on repeating his name but no words came out from him. His eyes dropped slowly and his fists clenched and unclenched simultaneously.

"You don't look well," she tried to push him into the bed. "Why didn't you tell me...I'll get something..."

"Don't try to pretend what you are not," he hit out with his words. "I really hate you...hate you...hate *you*..."

Tension swirled around Ria and every vein in her body turned numb at his words. Her heartbeats increased and every word of his stung like a poisoned dart. She closed her eyes tightly, knowing that what Arman felt for her was nothing but disgust...and hatred. She didn't know which emotion she could handle best. Why couldn't she just forget the whole thing and leave him alone? He was living a better life when she wasn't around, for sure. In fact, he had even tried to escape from her. She was the one who had subconsciously wanted to be with him. Maybe she was to blame for the plight he was in.

If only she could have stopped herself from falling in love with him, then leaving him would have been an option she would have chosen gladly.

14

"'Flu?"

Ria stared at the doctor, her mouth twisted grimly. She had left Arman in her room all day, thinking that he had fallen unconscious because of exhaustion after a busy day, but then he had completely passed out. It was a bright sunny day outside but for Ria it was filled with gloom and regret – regret that she had wasted so much time denying the love she had felt for him. Why did it always happen with her? She suffered from an inflated ego, she told herself ruefully.

She could hardly bear this suspense any longer. Why didn't he get up? Why did his face look so colourless?

"It's a kind of 'flu that comes up when in stress, Mrs Gupta. Maybe it's just due to odd working hours," the doctor said, trying to explain to the distraught woman. He didn't exactly know how to explain. All he had been doing since the past two hours was to answer Ria's endless queries.

"What kind of 'flu...," Ria began again. "Listen doctor, I really want to know...I can't leave my husband like this. He hasn't got up for..."

"I know, I know. He will be fine," he consoled her. "It seems as if he hasn't been taking care of himself well..."

Ria stared at the doctor as if he had grown two horns. "But he looked perfectly fine to me this morning..."

He shrugged and said in a placid voice, "It will pass Mrs Gupta. You have to give him plenty of liquids and see that you don't put him under any strain," he said, drawing his eyebrows solicitously. "You understand me?"

Ria nodded, suddenly anxious to get to Arman.

She found him on the bed, with his eyes closed tightly, his forehead beaded with sweat and a certain intensity on his face that almost scared her to death. She walked hesitantly towards the bed, petrified to be rejected if he found out that she was hovering near him. As far as she knew, Arman did not want her. It hurt her that he could not understand what turmoil was going on inside her. If he were to ask, she was sure that she would not have been able to answer him. The situation was too pensive to talk about.

If she was honest, not loving Arman was not an easy task, especially when he looked so sick. She should just forget that she was in love with him for the time being and concentrate on taking care of him.

She touched his forehead and found nothing unusual in the temperature, except for his face which didn't look like it used to a few days ago. She looked at him closely and saw how his eyelashes fringed softly around his beady eyes. His lips were curled a little as if he wanted to call out to something to ease his pain. His hair…

She reached to lift his head and pulled the thin band from his hair. It came out easily and the silkiness of his hair surprised her. Never had she found men to have such lovely texture. She guessed Arman wouldn't like to be told that. After all, no man liked to know that a girl liked the way he took care of his mane. His hair was shoulder length and she spread them carefully on the pillow, giving them room to breathe. How in God's name did he keep them tied all the time? He looked better when he left them open, she thought. A tender sigh escaped from her lips with love for him flowing like a broken dam.

Will he never get up? All she could think about was Arman never waking up. Why couldn't she get something positive to think about? She used to be a romantic person, loving the simple things of life and living life like a spoilt brat. Her main problem was she had never tried to come out of her cosy cocoon even when it was time for her to break free from it. She had been longing for something that wasn't even worth a dime.

She turned to look at Arman, who looked pale and feverish. She felt a lump arise in her throat and she wanted to cry out. She had failed to appreciate what she had been blessed with…

Just for a split second, her eyes flew towards Arman's frail body and she found him trying to say something she could barely hear. If only he would be the same Arman as he had been not so long ago…she couldn't just bear to see him like this.

Trying to harden her heart, she knew that feeling sorry for herself wasn't the right thing to do at that moment. All that was required was for her take the best possible care of Arman and after that…she took a deep breath, fate would have to decide.

Not for more than half an hour did Ria ever leave the room where Arman lay. She looked as if she needed a bed too. Except for her bloodshot eyes, no one could have guessed how agonising the situation was. Arman was not a patient that any doctor would love to have. He neither opened his mouth for medicine nor did he get up and sit up on bed. It was as if he didn't want to ever get up. He grew weaker as each day passed, but gradually the medicine started working on him. Ria's heart almost did a somersault when Arman opened his eyes, which stared unblinking at the ceiling. She thought of asking the doctor about this strange habit of his but after two days, Arman began to show improvement.

It was a severe bout of 'flu but the doctor had assured her that it would pass away…

Wasn't it taking way too much of time?

"Why don't you sleep for an hour at least?" her mother asked, when she went downstairs to take a quick breakfast.

"I have slept, Mom," Ria lied smoothly. Soon however, she spoiled it by yawning and blinking her sleep-filled eyes.

"Well, that said it all, didn't it?"

Ria managed a grim grin, "I can't sleep when my husband is suffering, Mom…I'm just waiting for his fever to break."

"What would be the use if you were to fall sick in the end?" Vidhya grumbled though surprised to hear her daughter refer to Arman as her 'husband'.

"Oh Mom, thanks for caring, but I'm perfectly fine!" Ria said, hugging her mother tightly. For a split second all her weariness seemed to have vanished. It was good to have a mother, especially one who gave advice without being asked.

"Arman would be fine, Ria..."

"I'm not finding him *fine*!" she said, pulling away. "I have to go."

"Tanvi had come to ask about you...," Vidhya began.

"I'll meet her when Arman is alright. We will go together," she said, planting a quick kiss on her mother's cheek. She swiftly departed from the room.

Vidhya couldn't believe her ears. Of all the things it was strange to see Ria so optimistic about her relationship with Arman! Could it be that her daughter was falling in love with Arman? The possibility was certainly worth sharing, especially with that nosy-poker husband of hers!

When Ria entered the room, she found the bed empty. At first she couldn't believe her eyes, so she quickly switched on the lights. Damn!

"Arman!" she yelled at the top of her voice.

"*Shush*!" she turned behind to find Arman standing at the entrance of the bathroom door, glaring at her, "I know what my name is."

"Uh...sorry," she said in a small voice, not knowing how to confront a somewhat normal Arman. He didn't look well but then she didn't think he wanted to know that.

"Why was I in bed? I should be in office," Arman said, muttering to himself.

"You were down with 'flu and...," Ria winced when Arman tripped as he took a step towards her. "And I think it would be better for you to be in bed."

Arman looked at her for more than a second, looking somewhat confused and in a disarray. Blinking, he seemed to be trying to grasp what Ria had said.

He wondered as to what was she doing with him? And it wasn't his apartment...for that matter, nothing looked familiar.

"I'm okay...but where am I?"

Ria shook her head, trying to make him stand, "I will tell you once you come and lie down on the bed."

"Come and lie down on the bed?"

Ria felt a faint blush creep over her cheeks. Damn it, she should have phrased her words in a proper manner. Even a sick Arman was an attractive Arman for her. And on top of it all, she was in love with him!

Way to go Ria!

"To rest," she emphasised.

"I can't move a muscle," he groaned as he tried to walk towards the bed. "And stop pulling on my arm, Ria!"

"Oops! Sorry. Did it hurt?"

"No, it's okay," but the paleness of his face contradicted his words. "I don't need to go to bed anyway..."

By the time he lay down, he felt as if he had reached heaven. Maybe he should close his eyes again for a few seconds. He wanted to ask Ria what she was doing there but couldn't find the right words or the strength to talk to her. So he decided to lie quietly till he felt better.

Ria could feel Arman retreating back into his shell. If only he were to specify how he felt then she wouldn't have felt so conscious about him. On seeing him awake, she felt she had acquired a spring in her feet.

But why couldn't she feel a little more comfortable?

"Why are you looking at me like that?" he asked dryly, raising a brow sarcastically.

"L...like what?"

"*Ahrggh*...don't be scared. I'm the last person you should be scared of."

Entwining her fingers together, Ria looked away from his probing eyes. "I don't know what you are talking about," she mumbled.

"Why are you here?"

"We are married," she stated the obvious as if that answered everything.

"*Ma*...!" Arman stared at her as if she had gone mad. "When..."

"When?" Ria narrowed her eyes, a little affronted. "You and I got married a week ago?"

For several seconds that turned into minutes, Arman didn't answer her question and Ria stood breathing hard, while trying to calm her distraught nerves. Why couldn't Arman remember their marriage? If he was deliberately trying to scare her, then he was succeeding, she thought. It was a frightening situation with Arman acting like a patient of amnesia.

Of course, if he wanted to forget her, then...Ria shook her head mentally, admonishing herself for being such a scared puss.

Arman's eyes closed again as if the strain of talking was too much for him to withstand.

"Maybe you should sleep...," she began.

"Lie down with me," he said suddenly, his voice sounding so tired that Ria felt a lump arise in her throat. .

Maybe he still wanted her, even if he did not love her.

He stretched out his hand to her and she didn't hesitate to clasp it in both of hers. His fingers convulsed in her palms, as if out of weakness. But she was surprised to find that for a sick man, he had enough strength to pull her down on the bed. She tried to move and give him enough space to lie down, but the moment his head touched the pillow, he was fast asleep. Trying to get up and pull her hand away, she failed. He was still too strong for her.

Well, she thought with a tired sigh, maybe it wasn't hurting him that much after all and sleeping in his arms was better than worrying about him all the time.

Ria was laughing with him.

They were walking down the green lanes of New York, hand in hand...with no one else in sight. It was a beautiful evening. He had plans to take her home that night, nourish her with good food around a candlelit balcony. It wasn't something originally romantic but she would love it, he thought, just as he loved her...

It was time for him to tell her that he loved her, wasn't it? Then he would propose to her formally. The ring he had bought for her would make her fall in love with him again. Of that he was sure. It was a beautiful ring, just as Ria was. Set in dark green emeralds and blood red rubies surrounding a diamond, just as she was a diamond in the darkness of the world.

That night her eyes shone when she wore the ring.

"Does that mean a 'yes'?" he asked eagerly, suddenly feeling like he was back in high school.

"Of course," she giggled, lowering her eyes as her lashes fell to cover her upper cheeks, trying to hide the glitter that was as bright as that of the ring. Then she looked up and said softly, "I love you Mike...I love you so much!"

Ria felt Arman move restlessly and then he was yelling something she couldn't decipher. As she turned, she noticed that Arman was sweating profusely. Her heart missed a beat when she saw the look on his face. It was filled with pure hatred and disgust.

"What are you doing here?" his words were rough and meant to insult.

"Arman..."

"Just get out of my sight!"

Ria felt as if she had been sent to the gallows though she held her body tight, forcing herself to breathe normally, "Care to tell me what I have done?"

"You...," Arman sat up on the bed and groaned due to a heavy head. "*Oh God...!* It was a nightmare," he groaned.

Ria put out her hand and touched his forehead, but Arman pushed it away. She wasn't a girl who could bear to be rebuffed, but suddenly she didn't care how much Arman hated her. She was prepared to lick her wounds in solitude but the uppermost thought in her mind was to see him get alright.

"Just lie down, will you?" she said in a firm voice, "and no...I'm not going to take another word from you."

"As if I'm listening to you!" he shot back. "Didn't I ask you to get out of my sight?"

"*Shush!*" she soothed him, her fingers entangled in his long hair. "I'm listening to you. I'll get out of your sight as soon as you close your eyes."

He stared at her as if she could win the title 'Miss Liar'. He asked, "Why should I close my eyes?"

"To sleep," she replied softly.

He lay back without knowing and said while staring at her face, "You still love him, don't you? No matter what I do for you...actually I haven't done anything for you at all. Forced you into a loveless marriage and then took you to bed as if you belonged to me...but you don't, do you?"

"Go to sleep, Arman...," Ria bit her lower lip hard, hoping that the physical pain would dull the pain he felt inside.

"You don't, do you?" he repeated.

"Don't what?"

"Belong to me."

I belong to you! You...you...you!

His eyes were already closed and an answer to his question was impossible. She couldn't let him know how vulnerable she was to his apparent animosity. Maybe when he was better, she would tell him about her feelings for him. He might be more rational about it, but then who cared?

They were married; maybe Arman would honour the scared vows they had taken.

"You didn't answer my question?" he asked all of a sudden when she thought he had dropped off to sleep.

"Maybe this will," she said with a gentle smile and bent down to touch his lips. It was supposed to be just a touch but Arman's lips captured hers, catching her unawares.

"Hmm…Arman…wait…"

"No…don't wait."

Yes, don't wait!

What had she got to lose? The mere touch of him was like reaching heaven. But what about the uncompromising attitude that Arman showed towards her? Would making love to him make any difference?

Slowly she told herself that her mind was playing tricks with her body as her thoughts desired what was natural. She looked at Arman's troubled face and thought of giving in for he was her husband after all. The most important thing was that she was in love with this man.

She moved her fingers over his muscled body and rested her head on his chest, "Arman, do you love me?"

It was an inappropriate question to ask when all Arman felt was hatred for her. Maybe it was temporary or it could even be forever. She felt a sudden fear enveloping her heart. Would she never get to live with the man she loved?

He did not respond to her question though. His hands stopped moving and he turned his head away from her, "I think I should sleep."

Ria felt like dying. Arman had done the ultimate thing – he had rejected her touch and…her feelings. If that was not humiliation enough, then she didn't know what else could be. They were husband and wife, yet they didn't behave like one. She walked out of the room, her face so downcast and miserable that her mother hovered around her for a long time. He thought she was still in love with Mike.

She remembered the horrible encounter she had had with his wife. Didn't Mike's wife tell her what a fool she had been? She could still hear the words ringing in her ears. They were so loud and sharp that she got up crying.

"I didn't know he was married!"

Clarisse, a beautiful blond, curled her red lips maliciously, "Even if you had known, I'm sure you wouldn't have left him alone." Walking threateningly towards her, she had almost spit out, "A slut likes to paw on all men... married or unmarried!"

She had stood silent, absolutely pale and out of her mind at hearing those words. She wasn't like that! She was not a slut!

"I wish you would watch your words...," Ria began in an amiable tone.

"You are a bitch. Do you know that Ria? And I want you to keep your hands off my husband!"

And she had. She had avoided all the places she knew she could find him in. Even though Mike's calls were insistent, she had ignored him. The trauma of confronting his wife again was something she didn't want. Mike had left her alone for a week as he hadn't wanted to face another woman's tantrums. This was the excuse that he had cited for keeping away from her. She had been completely shattered but being mentally strong, she had camouflaged her feelings behind a cold look. What had shocked her was that she had been already engaged when all this happened!

And now she was married to a man who thought of her in the same way as Clarisse did. She hated herself at that moment. How could she end up in a situation like she was in?

Tears filled her eyes and she let them flow freely as she needed to give vent to her feelings which she had kept pent up for long. When the sobs grew insistent and would not stop, Ria lay back on her bed, waiting to get over her emotions. She didn't like feeling so weak and unwanted in love. She wished she had never fallen for Mike; she also wished she had never fallen for Arman either!

But Mike was her past and she had come to accept it. Why couldn't Arman do the same?

There was a knock on her door and she quickly wiped away her tears.

"Ria... it's me, Tanvi. Can I come in?"

"Oh...," she said, disappointed that Arman hadn't bothered to come and meet her. However, Ria called out, "Yes, sure. Come in."

Tanvi walked in hesitantly, her face clouded with worry, "I could hear you crying. What's wrong?"

Ria couldn't answer and what could she possibly say? That she was thinking about Arman and crying? That she was thinking how Arman was unable to love her?

"Say something," Tanvi's voice prodded her gently. "You know I care for you. If there is something you want to share, I'm always there."

"Yes...," Ria's voice choked, her throat tightening. "Thank you for saying that. Of late I have been feeling as if no one loves me."

"Hey!" Tanvi moved forward to hug her. "You silly girl, have you had a fight with Arman?"

"He doesn't care," Ria broke into uncontrollable sobs. "And I can't force him to either."

"You have not been married long, Ria," Tanvi reminded her. "I know it hasn't been a fairytale for you since it was imposed upon you by your parents." Looking far with a disturbed glaze, she continued, "You seemed such a perfect match."

"No, nothing can be perfect, Tanvi, in my life," Ria said in a faint voice. "I was born to a man who left my mother like a coward. I was brought up by a man who imposed his rules upon me. I was thrust upon a man who wants to impose his rules upon me. Isn't that an irony of fate?"

Tanvi felt sorry for Ria. Yes, it hadn't all been a fairytale for Ria. She had met Ria's biological father long ago and he had been a jerk through and through. Amitab Melhera wasn't one though, but he had an approach of doing what he considered to be right. Most of the times, his views had turned out to be nothing short of a disaster.

"You are unhappy with Arman," Tanvi stated quietly.

"No…not unhappy," Ria sighed and pulled away. "Maybe I'm a person who is dissatisfied with whatever good I get in life. I have been given the best of education and so much freedom that I've misused it all…"

Tanvi filled up with dread on hearing these words for she considered Ria to be a feisty girl. It was as if Ria was giving up on herself.

"…I'm not a good person, am I, Tanvi?"

"No!" Tanvi sighed harshly. "Talking like this would get you nowhere, Ria. Tell me what the problem is? I might be able to help you."

"Arman hates me," Ria stated candidly. "He was not the first man in my life, so he is unable to bear that."

"Ever wondered why he is unable to bear that?"

Ria looked at Tanvi with empty eyes, "What's there to wonder about? He wanted a virgin, which I'm not."

Tanvi gulped at that piece of news silently. Now that was something she hadn't known despite being so close to Ria. But what had been done was done; there was no use in crying over spilt milk. Digging graves would only bring pain to everyone and Ria already sounded so guilty, blaming herself and her lifestyle...a positive road to depression.

"Virginity doesn't matter Ria as long as you don't label it as the ultimate. You should always take every incident in your life as a challenge. Whatever has happened to you happens to many people. What makes you strong is how you come out of an unpleasant situation. That's life. You can't make any compromises with life."

Ria shook her head, "I feel so ashamed all of a sudden. I didn't even wait for the right man to come into my life."

15

Arman got up with a severe headache. He could vaguely remember talking to Ria about something, but what it was he couldn't recall. Although the headache increased, he felt stiffness all over his body. The pain in his soul kept on nagging him. What was the reason for the pain?

His wife didn't care for him. Ria had never been interested in him, even if she seemed to be so during his illness. The only difference between them was that they were legally bound by marriage. However, that could be resolved any moment though. There was no way he was going to let Ria suffer by forcing himself upon her. They were not meant to be together after all.

Getting up and feeling as if he had been shot twice, Arman found his way to the washroom. After ten minutes he emerged, his eyes a little less red and his lips pursed in a determined line. He pulled his hair back into place as he hopped into his jeans and shirt. He intended to break the news gently to her. He had suffered from 'flu earlier too but never so seriously. He couldn't even recall how many days he had wasted lying in bed.

As he walked along the corridor, he heard noises from the room adjacent to his. It was the room he had occupied when he had come here for the first time. He felt it was best if they stayed away from each other.

He was about to enter the room when he heard Ria sobbing.

"If you want, I will talk to him," Tanvi was saying.

"What would be the use? I don't want to talk to him. He is lower than a snake's belly! I regret the day when I first laid my eyes on him!"

Arman stood with every muscle in his body frozen. Is that what she thought about him?

"I wish Dad had never sent me to New York and to see him after...," the bitterness in her voice became more pronounced.

For a second Arman felt tempted to storm in and confront his wife. He wondered how he could have come to love *this* woman who compared him with a snake – a woman who didn't even care to discuss that she had a problem with him? Since that was the case, there was no point in talking things over. It was silly to even think that they had a future together.

He slammed the door open, forgetting the need to knock first but went and stood in the doorway, throwing daggers at the woman who had been his life once.

"Arman! What are you doing here?" he heard Ria exclaim in the most affectionate voice she had ever used with him.

"How many times I have told you not to pretend that you care for me?" he growled, enunciating every word with venom. "I knew you have hated me, but I didn't know you hated me so much."

"Uh…Arman…," Tanvi got up, her eyes pleading with him to be quiet. "What are you talking about?"

"Please Tanvi, I appreciate your coming over and having a talk with my wife (the way he used the word *wife* made Ria wince) but I think I'll take over now and hear personally what she thinks about me."

"She loves…," Tanvi began but stopped when she met Ria's eyes, which pleaded with her to remain silent. Maybe she wanted to tell him herself, she thought. "Tanvi you go. I think Arman wants to talk to me."

"She took care of you…," Tanvi pleaded again.

"Tanvi!" Ria's mouth turned hard. "I asked you to leave."

For a moment Arman didn't understand and his eyes darted from Ria to Tanvi and back. She had taken care of him? Had he heard it right? Did it mean anything now when everything had been lost? If he had hoped to see her love him, then he was merely living in a fool's paradise. Maybe he should have done what Ria actually wanted as there was no point in prolonging the agony.

Shrugging and yielding to the demands of the situation, Tanvi got up to leave. She glanced at Arman and seeing his nasty look, thought it would have been better if Ria left with her. Arman hardly looked pleasant or in the mood for a discussion.

As soon as the door closed behind him, Arman turned and locked it firmly to avoid any interruption. Frowning, Ria could only watch silently. Seeing him walk around pleased her, but seeing his look, she knew it was time for her to squirm and make her escape from his presence.

"So you think I hate you?" she asked softly, watching his face grow tense. "And you think I pretend to care about you?"

"Please stop all that nonsense!" said Arman, digging his hands into his pockets and staring hard at her. "I heard what you just now said about me in clear and loud words."

"What...what did I say?"

"That I'm lower than a snake's belly...."

When Ria opened her mouth to deny vehemently, he laughed roughly, "You never lied to me Ria; you don't need to lie now either."

"But..."

"If you would care to listen, I want to tell you something," he said, walking determinedly towards her. "After that you can decide what you want to do."

She didn't look the same as she had a few days ago. *Did she not look pale and devoid of all colour? Why would he care now?* Why *should* he care now?

"Are you listening to me?" he asked smoothly.

Ria sat stiffly, hurt at the tone of his voice. There was insult in every syllable. She nodded, every nerve stung tight.

"Our marriage was a mistake right from the beginning," he began, his throat suddenly going dry. "I foolishly thought that perhaps we could work out something together, but it seems like we couldn't. We are two poles apart. I guess for a good relationship, any kind of relationship for that matter, you need love and respect, but we keep blaming each other and have no love lost between us. Whatever fondness we had for each other, I find it is now fading away and getting replaced with the word *hate*. I don't want that..."

"I don't hate you Arman," Ria whispered, her eyes pleading. "And I don't think our marriage is a..."

"Nothing is going to change my mind now," he cut in. "I will go back to New York as soon as possible..."

"But you are not feeling well!"

"I may feel better once I am away," he agreed, "because that's the only hope left for my peace of mind now."

Ria literally gasped, "I think you are right. You should go."

Arman eyed her sharply, "So it's okay with you?"

Ria looked away, biting her lower lip, "Of course."

"I was not wrong then," he turned away to leave her alone.

She stopped him, "Wrong about what?"

"You don't care."

Ria swallowed the tears that were wanting to flow down, "Yes Arman, I don't care. I don't love you. I don't want to live with you...you are right about everything."

"You forgot to add something else."

Ria waited.

"You are still in love with Mike. You still want to be with him; after all he was your first..." he stopped abruptly.

"Why did you stop?" Ria got up, her eyes flashing while her heart died with every word that she uttered. "He was the first man I loved; he was the first man I cared about and he was the first man I slept with, right?"

Arman heard her and didn't like it the way she pronounced each and every word. "Of course that makes me a 'no go' zone for any man and especially a man like you. Am I denying that?" Ria pursed her lips. "No I'm not! You go your way, I'm not stopping you, Arman Gupta. I would have been acceptable if I had been a virgin, but..."

"I never said that..."

"Do you have anything else to say?" she cut in ruthlessly.

"Yes...," he took a long breath. "I'll send in the divorce papers as soon as I reach New York."

16

"Terminating the contract?" Amitab Melhera stared at Arman as if he had gone mad. "Do you know I have commitments with my clients? I need the designs now, Arman."

"I'm leaving your daughter," Arman informed him. "If you are willing to continue still with our business dealings, I am agreeable."

"*What*?"

"You heard me," Arman said, not wanting to arouse a father's temper. "It was a mistake right from the very beginning."

Arman didn't want to reveal his pain when saying that. How could he ever face himself now? How could he face his wife…?

"She took care of you, you know…"

"Anyone would have done it," Arman shot back.

"You thankless little scum! No one would have done it the way she did it for you," Amitab looked furious.

Arman just shrugged, "We are not meant to be together."

"What now then?" Amitab's voice grated.

"I'm going back. If you want, you can take the entire contract with you…"

"No," Amitab just stopped himself from yelling. "We will finish this one. Of course, it's understood that I don't want to see your face again."

Arman smiled sadly, "I know."

"*Then get out*," Amitab shouted, his voice far from normal.

Arman did exactly that. He had expected blows from his father-in-law but all he got was bitter contempt. Maybe he deserved it for he was filled with contempt for himself too. The mere thought of his relationship with Ria could only fill with self-disgust. Well, maybe it was better than being stuck in a marriage that was nothing but a farce.

Four months later

"Dinner?"

Arman thought about it for a long second until he heard the speaker spell out the words again.

"Dinner, why?"

"So that you can survive?" Christina told him sassily, laughing like a little girl. The day she had come to know that Arman had come back for good, she had planted herself in his life again.

Arman was no longer interested in her. All day he had been hoping to have a talk with his father. It had been a long day just as it had been long four months away from Ria. He didn't know why he still thought about her. After all, he had willed himself not to love her any more. She didn't, so why did he feel depressed?

That self-explanatory statement seemed futile as he had to live and to live, he had to forget her.

"Come on Arman, it's the third time I'm asking you out and all you do is to brood," her voice came from afar. "You know I have lots of other things to do..."

"And I have to do lots of other things too Chris..."

"You don't have a wife now. What's keeping you so busy? Another girlfriend?"

"Chris...," Arman leaned back on his chair, feeling tiredness creep over him. "You are just a pain in my neck and it would be only to your own good if only you were to accept this fact."

"How *dare*..."

"I always did," he replied smoothly and switched his mobile off for good.

As soon he threw his mobile aside, Jeevan Gupta came in, his eyes sad with worry. He looked older than he was, "Why did you call me?"

"You know why," Arman said with a slight exasperation. "Every week I plan to go to the lawyer you end up taking the task...on the whole, I never get a result."

"*Hmmm...*," Jeeven Gupta sat down on a chair and eyed his son with concern. "The lawyer has gone on a holiday or something."

"Last month you said it was his daughter's wedding. Has he now gone on a honeymoon himself?"

Jeeven tried to laugh but coughed instead, "*No*!"

"Have you shown yourself to the doctor?"

His father shook his head, "No time; I was busy with your lawyer. He took the fee and decided that he needed a holiday that he had been craving for."

"*You*...," Arman just couldn't believe his ears. "Am I still in New York? Things happen promptly here, for God's sake!"

"You didn't get married here, so the process is taking longer than needed," the father lied effortlessly, hiding the fact that he had sent the lawyer away to prevent Arman from seeking the divorce.

Arman sighed roughly, "So how much time?"

Jeeven knew what his son was asking for – how much more time to get a divorce, but he never used the word as if he found it repulsive. Then why go through it?

Suddenly he felt he didn't know his son at all. The Arman he knew had got somehow lost somewhere. That's how he would describe Arman – *lost*. Apart from the business decisions, Arman wasn't interested in anything. Most of the time he found him brooding or pondering with a frown on his face.

"Amitab rang me up today," Jeevan said. Arman's ears perked up, "Ria is not doing well..."

Arman didn't ask anything. He knew his father would say whatever he wanted to say and he didn't want to enter into any argument. They had a royal tiff as soon as Arman had returned from India.

"I hope you didn't leave her pregnant," his father said casually.

"*Dad!*"

"Well?"

"Well what?" Arman snapped.

"Did you?"

"*No*!"

"Good thing that you didn't use her too," his father spelled out crudely. "You have been in and out with many women by now and so far no one has told you that, I suppose?"

"You didn't have a problem before."

"I'm a stupid old man. No one would even listen to what I have to say," Jeevan reasoned logically. "But I mean whatever I say."

"I didn't use her, as you so sweetly put it," Arman clarified. "We...," he stopped talking abruptly as images of Ria sliding against him flashed. The last time he had slept with her was when he was sick. Why did that keep cropping up in his mind now? How could she have slept with him when he was sick? Somehow he could not erase her image from his mind. It must have been a powerful hallucination because she had become a permanent fix on his mind. Damn it! Of all the things he had to remember her now, he cursed.

"What's wrong?"

Arman looked up and found his father scrutinising him stealthily. "What could be wrong, Dad?"

"You are changing colour."

"A mere human tendency."

Jeeven shook his head, "What do you want me to do?"

"Find another lawyer..."

"Why don't you ask Ria to manage the divorce papers?"

Arman winced painfully at the word. Even her name

caused a bitter sweet discomfort inside. "Because I told her that I would do it."

"Well, you better not talk to her. She is not in the condition to face it anyway," he got up, coughing a little. "I think I need a holiday from all this."

Arman eyed his father suspiciously and agreed wholeheartedly, "You are taking things too much upon yourself. You need a break."

"Of course I want you to get a divorce," Jeevan answered sweetly, turning his back on his only son, while muttering under his breath, "*and I'd rot in hell first!*"

As soon as his father left his office, Arman picked up his phone to dial the number he thought he had forgotten.

"Yes?"

"Is Ria Gupta around?"

There was a significant pause and Arman swallowed hard when he realised it was Ria who had picked up the phone.

"No one calls me that."

Her voice sounded rough and dry and very tired.

"I heard you were not feeling well."

Another pause...during that pause, Arman waited desperately to hear her utter something. When she did, her voice came out only a little firmer, "No, I'm doing fine. It might be the monsoon. I'm still getting used to the weather."

"Oh!"

Did her voice sound a little wobbly? Arman wanted to ask more but was almost scared to do so. What if he said something that would reveal his true feelings?

"If you have finished asking, I have to go and do the dishes."

"*Dishes?*"

"Mom and Dad have gone out for the weekend."

"So where are the maids?"

"Given them a day off," she replied curtly. "her kids had Parents Day."

"*Whose* kids?"

"The maid's."

"Oh for God's sake...!" Arman couldn't believe what he was hearing. Ria had given the maids a day off because of a Parent's Day celebration?

"What? Do you have a problem with that?"

"Ria...," Arman tried to suppress his laugh, "what are you talking about?"

"Uh...sorry," her voice turned stiff again. "Why is it that you rang up?"

"*Ria*...," he began, suddenly missing her like one would miss a part of one's body.

"I'm doing fine, Arman."

Sighing, he left it at that. "Okay. Take care then..."

She didn't reply back and when he kept down the receiver, he felt an overwhelming emotion overcome his being. What was wrong with him?

He redialled the number but no one picked it up. When at last he had nearly given up and decided to keep the phone down, Ria picked up the receiver.

"What is it?" she asked tersely.

"Shouldn't you be in bed?"

"Doing *what*?"

"Resting?" Arman suggested coolly.

"Listen Arman, you just can't sit thousands of miles away and tell me what to do...," her breathing increased in anger. "And please don't call me again...!"

"Wait! Don't keep the phone down," he cleared his throat, speaking out slowly. "Uh..."

"Is it about the divorce?" her voice sounded unusually high pitched as if she was trying to control her voice and her feelings. "As far as I know, you didn't send me anything yet."

"The lawyer is on a holiday."

"The *lawyer*...!" disbelief sounded in her voice. "Then, hire another one."

"I'm trying," Arman bit, hurt that she didn't even want to talk about it or try to settle it. But then why would she? After all it was better to live apart than to hurt each other and call names.

"Then try harder," her voice didn't sound amiable either. "I would be glad to get over this as soon as possible."

Arman felt like throwing something, "Of course, I want the same thing..."

"Then I'll wait for them," she sounded as if she had enough of this conversation and before Arman could stop himself from cursing again, she added, "And Arman, you don't have to worry about it. I'm going to sign the papers..."

"What do you mean?"

There was a slight hesitation in her voice now, "You don't have to come and see to it personally, okay?"

Arman frowned, his brain cells clicking as if sensing something unusual but all he said was, "Of course."

She disconnected the phone and he didn't call back. After all, what was the use of calling up a woman who didn't even want to be called his wife? He had very little self-respect left as it was.

17

"That was a childish thing to do!" Amitab Melhera lashed out at his daughter, who stood there looking at him, her eyes saying a thousand words.

"I just want Arman to be happy," she tried to explain, her mouth twisted derisively. "If this is what he wants, he gets it."

"Since when have you begun to care about his happiness?" he argued, knowing that this was the last question that Ria wanted to hear. Maybe he was even hurting her, but what in the hell was he supposed to do? Admit that it had been a damn mess just because of him only?

Ria didn't budge, "I think I'll pass that question. If you want, I'll go all by myself. Sort some things out..."

"You don't want to live here in India?"

"I have to think about that, Dad. I have lived all my life in Buffalo; maybe a change from here would do me good."

"You are not in a condition to travel for God's sake!"

"I'm perfectly alright," she assured her father. She didn't think she needed to argue any more, for his sake and also for her own.

It had been one long day and she wanted it to end without arguing.

"Well, I don't believe you," Amitab turned his back to his daughter, closing his eyes. "But you can go, if that's what you want. You are right, you *do* need a change..."

"I'll go alone."

Amitab swung around, preparing to give her a dressing down that only Dads are capable of but words died on his lips when he saw tears in her eyes. "Fine!" he muttered.

Sighing with relief, Ria turned to leave and pack her things. She didn't really want to tell anyone that she didn't want to stay in Delhi. Her parental home held just too many memories and she was going mad with them. Her room didn't feel hers anymore. The smell of Arman and his presence were just too strong for her to endure. It was true that she had never given him any happiness when they were together and she didn't want him to suffer in a relationship that had no strong roots. What if she was in love with him? Whatever feelings he had for her were gone as soon as he came to know about her past. Did a woman's past matter so much to men? Couldn't they take it just like women did? Maybe it was just too much to ask and she didn't want to defend herself for her actions. There was nothing to defend in fact. Arman was welcome to his opinion about her and forcing him to change his mind was the last thing on her agenda. At that moment all she wanted was to get away…from herself, from her thoughts and from her conscience.

* * * * *

"She is not there, you mean?" a worried Amitab called up Arman to find out. Only he didn't get the response he wanted.

"You are right," came the reply.

"Then where is she?"

"How would I know? Wasn't she supposed to be living with you?" Arman said with irritation. How could she do this to him? Would escaping from him make him change his mind about the divorce? If she thought so, then she was wrong. After the way they had been dealing with each other, it was time that this sham was brought to an end.

"Who do you think then will sign the papers?" he almost spat out. Maybe he shouldn't have been so rude. After all, Amitab Melhera was still his father-in-law. Yet when he thought of how out of control the situation had gone, he couldn't control his temper.

"You will get them signed, okay?" he heard a tired voice.

What? Amitab Melhera giving up on him or what? After their business had got over, they had hardly kept in touch. In fact he hadn't thought of them and was neither interested in any business liaisons.

"Don't you at least want to see her before the divorce?"

"No," his answer was a final and there was nothing else to talk about.

Amitab Melhera put down the phone, hardly able to control his anger. He was famous for one, but he knew that anger could never work in a situation like the one he faced. If he wanted to achieve something, then he had to maintain his poise and carry on with what was left.

It hardly mattered though. Accepting a mistake was beyond his principles and he didn't think he could bear to see the look on his wife's face when he revealed to her how eager Arman was to get divorce.

The way things were going on, disaster was yet to come.

His daughter Ria was definitely pregnant! And he hoped she had reached safely.

* * * * *

"No, I have not come here to meet him," Ria informed the man in front of her.

He was old and very familiar to the man she loved. If she wasn't mistaken, he was her very own father-in-law.

"But I thought..."

His eyes resembled Arman's, she thought, trying to look as normal as possible. After all, she didn't have to show how she really felt about Arman.

"Then why have you travelled all the way?"

"I've some unfinished business here," she ventured hesitantly. "Don't worry, I've not come to see Arman."

"Worry? Me?" he wanted to laugh. "I would be worried if you didn't want to see him. Why don't you go and see him?"

"No...I...," Ria cleared her throat. "I really don't want to see him."

It was a blatant lie and Jeevan could sense it.

"I'm Arman's father."

"You both look alike and you didn't come for our wedding."

Jeevan laughed, "I know. I was advised not to travel…"

"I'm sorry. It doesn't matter anyway. You know we are parting ways," she said, avoiding his eyes.

"He is inside. Go," he patted her on her back, encouraging her and somehow she felt better and not alone any more.

Frowning, Jeevan tried to understand but all he could see was a girl who was very much in love and yet wouldn't say it aloud. It wasn't Arman's fault if he thought about it. Maybe it was fate that they had tampered with. Maybe they would have met eventually and then fallen in love!

Her eyes didn't reveal her thoughts and neither did her facial expressions. He wished everything had gone well with the poor girl. How he loathed the situation himself!

She sat tentatively at the edge of the chair, totally uncertain of the future. She knew why she had come though she was afraid that she would be denied the pleasure.

After a long silence Ria asked, "Do you think he would want to meet me?"

"He doesn't really want to, I guess?"

Ria face fell, "Yes, I know. But then, when did I care for what he wanted?" she mused silently. She fixed her gaze at Arman's office, "Is he busy?"

Jeevan managed not to grin, "I think you are going to see him even if he was."

"Damn right, I will!"

Arman was having a bad day. He had been nursing a very bad headache after having a long talk with his lawyer and just the thought of not seeing Ria forever hadn't gone down well with him. They couldn't meet for a year before the divorce. How ludicrous was that! Thank God, he wasn't a lawyer. He really didn't understand how he would have handled all that business-like discussion about divorce.

But it's for the best! For whom?

For both you and Ria.

He didn't know about Ria, but it definitely was not doing good to his sanity. He remembered the words that Ria had said and he stiffened with indignation. Was it just pride? He knew he was hurt that made him leave her. It was a drastic measure. He regretted it; maybe he would regret it all his life.

"Yeah, it was the right thing to do."

"Talking to yourself again, Arman?" Jeevan walked in with a huge grin on his lips that Arman didn't trust any more.

"I think it's time you went to the old age home," he said with a matching grin. "You think too much about me."

"You are my only son. I think it's my duty to *think* about you."

Arman laughed, "Dad, tell me what you want to say. If it is about Ria, then I'm not planning to change my mind. We are just not suited to each other. It was a mistake to marry her. Call it foolishness on my part."

"Then there is no point in my staying here," he heard a staunch voice behind his father and he stared widely at the woman who stood in front of him.

Ria!

Ria!

He got up slowly, his fingers clutching the desk as if trying to seek support to his weak legs. Maybe he was dreaming. Of course, he was dreaming!

But she looked so real. She had the same beautiful dimpled cheeks, the cherry red pouty lips and the voluptuous figure which made her a complete woman. But she didn't look as if she was feeling well. There were dark circles around her eyes as if she had been contemplating over her life for long hours at night and spending the days without much nutrition. But she did dress well. No more baggy clothes that hid her. That short skirt must have killed many guys all through the corridor and the white shirt only seemed to be bursting at the seams. Her breasts looked so full! He just stopped himself from touching her. He so desperately wanted to hold her; so badly that he could taste the pain in his mouth.

"Yes it's me. And no, you are not dreaming."

"This is a…surprise," he said, looking at her with shock.

"I wanted to talk to you but I don't want to waste your time," she almost retreated from his office. "I can come again if you so desire."

"No, *wait!*"

"Isn't it great that she's here?" Jeevan said brightly, knowing that neither seemed happy to see each other. To think that they were seeing each other after four months! Young people were really crazy!

"Dad, excuse us," Arman's eyes pleaded to him to stay quiet. His father was close to shouting but controlled himself. He looked so damn happy!

"Okay, I know when I'm not wanted."

Ria walked in and stood pointedly in front of him, her eyes lowered as if trying to come to terms with herself.

"Sit down," he said woodenly before adding softly, "please."

"No, it's okay. I'm not here to sit. I wanted to talk…"

"Yeah sure. We can do that," Arman knew what she was going to say. He would hate each word but he was prepared to listen. But he could delay it as long as possible; as long as she sat in front of him.

"Arman…," she began, a little choked as if uncertain.

"How's everyone at home?"

His words were rushed and Ria frowned in confusion, "Everyone is fine. I wanted to say…"

"How come you travelled so far? You must be tired. Did you sleep for some hours before you…"

"I didn't feel a thing. Thank you for asking. I have been here since the past two days," she said, walking two steps closer to Arman that he could inhale her fragrance. The perfume she wore smelled of a faint mixture of roses and musk, but he really couldn't decipher. Whatever it was, she smelled so pure and looked so beautiful. He had felt an insane attraction before, but the separation had made him desperate and he noticed everything about her. He wanted to feel everything, anything about her.

"Then I'll order coffee for you," he said, moving his hand towards the intercom, but she moved faster and placed her hand on his to stop him.

He forgot to breathe then. Looking up, he met her frantic eyes, "You don't like coffee?"

"I don't care a damn! Arman, you are not listening to me!"

"We have a lot of time, baby. Just have a little patience."

"I don't have any," she mumbled, silenced at his sweet words.

But he had to know before she lost the courage, "You don't look well, Ria. Okay we will talk."

Thank God, she breathed a sigh of relief and took her hands off. Arman didn't like that.

Had to get used to not touching her!

There was so much to say, yet she couldn't understand why she had come all the way to tell him that. It could have been done easily over the phone without any hassles of having to face his reaction. But then somewhere inside her heart, there was a small wish that he would be thrilled at the words...

"I'm pregnant and I'm leaving," she paused for a breath. "I have got a job at West Seneca West Senior High School. I will be working there till I settle down."

Arman looked at her with disbelief!

"Arman...I said...," she didn't continue. There was no reason to as he had slumped back in his chair, his eyes wider than ever.

"Come again?"

Come again?

After what she had said, all he could say was *come again*?

"Four months pregnant, alright? And it's your baby by the way," she said, her spirit back for the moment. "In case you are thinking of any other way...," when he still didn't say anything, she continued, "I'm not asking you to stop the divorce..."

"Then what are you asking me to do?"

Isn't he going to say anything else? Her heart bled at his words as they sounded so casual, as if he really didn't care.

"I just wanted to tell you. I don't want..."

"You don't want the child?" he asked lightly, his brows knitting together.

A reaction at last!

"Did I say that? I'm saying that I'm pregnant!" she yelled, her chest heaving at the impact.

Arman got up a little jerkily as his worried eyes landed over her stomach. She looked at him, her eyes dejected than ever and feeling utterly depressed at his reaction. She wanted to cry but all she did was to stare.

"Why didn't you tell me before?"

"I seemed to be suffering from a guilty conscience. Although you don't deserve to be informed about this, but you are going to be a father."

"Ria...," Arman closed his eyes and sighed. "We didn't use protection, did we?"

"Who cared at that time?"

Her statement made him want to laugh, though he curbed his smile. Ria, the woman he loved more than anything, was bearing his child and she didn't even bother to hide it from him. Women in her case would have either aborted or disappeared, but she was brave and willing to go ahead singlehanded.

"I asked you to sit down. You already have strained yourself unnecessarily by travelling all the way. You really have to be mad!"

"Yes I'm mad; mad in love with you! It wouldn't matter to me even if I died. I see that it wouldn't matter to you in the least as to what happens. You keep on repeating that our marriage was a mistake!"

Arman turned a little ashen though he had a powerful urge to gather her in his arms and forget whatever differences they had.

Ria wanted to be held in his arms but saw that he made no move to do so. He looked so different when he wasn't in a good mood.

"When?"

"Maybe our wedding night…I wasn't planning to make love to you…"

"No, I mean…," he swallowed, "when did you fall in love with me?"

Ria narrowed her eyes, her lips dry all of a sudden before saying softly, "I always did and I didn't like it when you left."

"Oh *baby*…!" He gritted his teeth as if trying to shun away the pain. His eyes misted mysteriously and Ria drew in a sharp breath.

She leaned over to touch his sleeve, but he turned faster and took her in his arms. The impact of his nearness melted her, melted all the tears she had shed, melted all the pain she had nurtured inside.

"Oh, Arman, why did you leave me?" she whimpered.

"I don't know…I'm so scared to let you go now."

The admission made the tears swirling in her eyes to fall drop by drop and suddenly she was sobbing loudly. Her whole body shook as if wanting to forget how much she had missed him. She wondered if he had ever missed her though she had managed to convince herself that it didn't matter.

This time she had fallen head over heels in love and the pain of unrequited love was unbearable…

"Can't we stay together?" she asked.

Arman was breathing hard and he pulled away a bit to gaze deeply into her tear-filled eyes. "If only you were to stop crying, then I can think about it," he said, grinning from ear to ear. But she felt as if it was a forced grin.

"Think about it?" she teased him. "How much time will you take to *think*?"

"Uhhh...," he touched her cheeks, wiping away the wetness with his fingers, "what about the divorce?"

Ria froze and jerked away from him.

He was immediately apologetic, "Ria, no…"

"You seem too eager for a divorce," her eyes flashed. "Why? Are you sleeping around again?"

"It's not that!"

"Don't want to be burdened with a pregnant woman?"

"Damn it Ria, that's not fair!"

"I'm leaving. I just came here to give you the news," and she turned and walked away; walking as fast as her feet could carry.

Arman stared at her, his heart in his mouth, *"I love you, don't go!"*

She stopped then, but didn't turn. He waited, his heart beating crazily, yet he was scared – too scared to let her go.

"I'm not sleeping around Ria. I haven't touched a woman since I met you…"

"What about Christina?"

He took a step towards her, "She means nothing to me. It's you, I love. It's you, I want. It's you, I want to grow old with. It's you I crave for!"

Her palms gathered into tight fists at each word of his and she turned slowly, tears shimmering like silver in her eyes, "What…what about the divorce then?"

"You tell me what you want?"

"I want to be with you. I want to raise my child with you," she said simply.

"Anything!" he opened his arms for her and she went in as if she had never left.

Their lips met for a second, just to acknowledge each other's presence and then both were drowned in uncontrollable passion – so hot, so scorching that Ria felt her legs giving way. "Arman…"

"Do you really want to talk now?"

A giggle passed her lips. It was a ridiculous reaction, yet it felt good. She pointed out, "It's your office!"

"They can't see anything from outside," he said, his lips licking her throat. They felt wet and hot…just as she felt inside.

He carried her gently to his desk and held her against it, his hips moving in a sensuous dance as his fingers dealt with her shirt. Her breasts looked so ripe and so tempting that he wanted to suckle them. Her bra was something he had never considered a barrier. As he pulled it up, her nipples tightened up so hard that she groaned at the pain. But the sweetest pain was yet to come. As his lips took one of her nipple between his teeth, she held his head softly, letting him savour her as much as he could.

"A…Arman…I want…"

"Hmm, what do you want?" he mumbled.

"More."

"Oh God!" his hands slipped down. "I love your skirt. Makes you look like a sexy bombshell."

"I'm not sexy..."

"Aren't you?" he raised his left brow wickedly, curving his body with her. "Look, we fit perfectly..."

"You are too tall," she laughed and then she heard the maddening beat of his heart that matched hers.

"We fit," he reiterated. He wanted to kiss her again but she resisted. If someone were to enter, it would have made the situation awkward, but he loved her for her unpretentiousness. But he couldn't let go now; he had lived too long without her. He had felt so incomplete until that moment.

"Ohh...*don't...*"

"You are saying the wrong word, darling...says *yes*!"

Just then they heard a knock on his door. They froze and closed their eyes together in pain. The pleasure had been denied. Not a very good omen when they had just got together.

"I want to speak to Arman! Now!"

Ria raised her brows when she heard a familiar voice.

"Seems like your Chris is here."

18

"Damn, damn, damn!"

He moved to cover her naked breasts, buttoning her quickly and efficiently. Ria on the other hand didn't make any attempt to dress herself. There was nothing to say at the moment and Arman prayed that Chris would disappear to another planet. But when did God hear him?

Chris marched right in. "Oh, so you are with her!"

Ria folded her arms around her chest, "Yes, he is with me. You have any problem?"

"I'm not speaking to *you*," Chris snapped.

"Chris! She's my *wife,* for God's sake!" Arman said, putting his arm around Ria's shoulders. Protecting her further, he added, "And this is not the way to enter my office. If it was something important, you should have taken an appointment!"

"You bastard! When you were away from her, you

wanted me and now that you have her, you are throwing me away?"

"I never wanted you and *who* let you in?" he demanded, his eyes turning furious at her words.

"Some Mike...," she said vaguely.

Ria blinked at her ex-boyfriend's name, looking at Arman, "You didn't fire him?"

"Oh, now she decides who stays and who goes?"

"Just tell me what you have to say and leave!" Arman said, exercising great control over his emotions. Ria noticed he was trying to deal with her as patiently as he could, without losing his temper.

Chris started crying and Arman rolled his eyes, "What is it now, Chris?"

"I thought I'll marry you after you got rid of her."

"He will not get rid of me."

Her eyes dried automatically, "He doesn't love you!"

"I'm going to have his baby," Ria told her clearly.

"*What*? This is so disgusting."

"You can leave now," Arman came forward. "What is disgusting is the way you are making an issue out of this thing. Ria and I are back together and I don't want to say anything more."

"What's happening?" Jeevan Gupta entered, frowning at Chris.

"You son has crossed his limits!"

"Oh, back to Ria, is he?" Jeevan gleefully asked. "Oh, I'm so glad!"

"Because you are going to be a grandfather," Chris spitted viciously.

"What? I knew something was wrong!" Jeevan paused for a second and then laughed, "I'm happy anyway." He turned to Chris, "Don't be a fiddle between the two. If you are so eager to date, I'm always ready."

"Mr Gupta!"

"I'm not that old, you know," Jeevan wriggled his brows teasingly.

"I'm leaving!"

"I'll escort you," Jeevan offered and escorted her out of the office before she could say another word.

Ria shook her head at the absurdity of the situation, looking at Arman, giving him a typical wife-like look.

"I have not been sleeping with her!" Arman rushed to explain.

"Did I ask you?"

"Then don't look at me that way."

Ria shifted to her left leg. "How am I looking at you? Do you think you could help me sit on this desk? I'm too short."

Arman lifted her with ease and placed her on his desk without much ado. "I'm even afraid to say what you are thinking."

"I'm thinking about kissing you."

"Oh?"

Her fingers started unbuttoning his shirt, "I'm thinking about taking your clothes off," she said.

Arman's throat dried, "I'm thinking about touching you everywhere...kissing you everywhere..."

"Oh God...!"

He saw her put her hands inside his shirt and it felt like hot satin, "Now, are you helping me or shall I do it myself?"

"Do what?"

Her fingers cupped the back of his head, pulling him closer. Her lips covered his ears and gave him a long wet kiss. He whispered, "I want to make love to you," and he moved forward to kiss her when she pulled away a little, "but you have to do something for me..."

"What?" he mumbled, aching with desire to be one with her.

"Fire Mike."

"My, my, you are ruthless," he chuckled, knowing how important it was for her. "You always get what you want, don't you?"

"*I want you.*"

He almost gave in, but he still didn't feel it was the right moment. He said, "No, wait..."

Ria pulled back at the sudden tension in his voice, "What's wrong, Arman?"

"We are not going to do this," he said, fully aware of the soft contours of her body still clinging to his. "Let's talk first."

"You want to *talk*...now?" she moved away from him, looking worried. "You don't want me?"

"Of course, I want you, silly!" he smiled which thrilled her all over. "I have been such a jerk all this time...I want to tell you why I left you."

Ria felt her body stiffen at those words. She really didn't want to talk about that horrible time and how she had suffered without Arman...

"I heard you speaking to Tanvi and telling her how much you hated me..."

"But…oh God, Arman…I should have told you. I was telling her about Mike. I had realised how much you meant to me. I had been too arrogant, blaming you all the while."

Arman's throat constricted at her words, "You mean that?"

"Yes!" she cupped his face, looking deep into his eyes as if trying to connect his soul to her.

"I want to make up…," Arman began.

"Make up…? Arman, are you alright? We *are* making up for the lost time."

"I'm feeling perfectly fine," he grinned as he lifted her off the table, rejoicing at her very presence. "I'll take some days off and we shall go on our honeymoon."

"Honeymoon?" she asked with wonder in her eyes. "A real one?"

"Obviously. We will walk on the sands, watch the sun set, sit on the beach and let the waves welcome us…"

"That's poetic…"

"No," he swallowed, because the moment was just too profound. "That's love."

"And will you cry when I die?"

His arms tightened, almost bruising her, "You will not die!"

She traced her lips over the rim of his ears and whispered into his ears. He groaned as he closed his eyes in ecstasy, but this ecstasy was something more than mere lust. It was like a splash of happiness mixed with deep devotion. How had he come to live so far without her, he couldn't tell. Maybe love had changed it all…maybe the hunger in his heart would finally be appeased in her arms.

* * * * *

"Why didn't you tell Chris anything?"

They were lying on his bed in his New York apartment when he popped the question. Ria was lying on his chest, resting her face over his chest. It felt safe that way. His hands caressed her naked back and she sighed deeply. He was tempted to go further but he didn't. He liked being close to her. Sex wasn't a priority any more, for love had come to replace it.

Although he couldn't help feeling her wetness…maybe he should…

"I didn't feel like…," her voice came out unsteadily.

"You didn't even argue," he murmured and got a light twitch on his nipple for it. "Ouch! I meant, maybe Chris was fishing for an argument."

"Your father was enough to handle her and now I don't want to talk about her."

Arman rolled on his back and she gave a small yelp in surprise. She peered down on his face to see if everything was alright and the smile on his lips told her so. She smiled back brilliantly and at that moment nothing mattered. "You want to tell me why you seem so happy?"

"I can't believe I'm with you."

Ria narrowed her eyes, "Why? Do you want to be with someone else?"

"Ria!" Arman gave a shout of laughter. "You act so damn jealous and you ask me not to."

Ria twisted her lips and looked away, "At least I don't leave you…"

"Hey!" his fingers came up and framed her chin, "I'm really sorry for that sweetheart…I was hurt. I have never felt this way with anyone else. I was scared to give a free hand to my emotions…" When she didn't smile, he went on, "Do you forgive me for my past dalliances?"

"Hmm…I have to," Ria told him simply. "I have not been close to perfect either. The mistake I committed was to get emotionally involved. I wish I were a man sometimes! It wouldn't have hurt this much then."

"Who told you men don't feel hurt…?" There was a sadness lurking in his eyes as he said, "It hurts Ria…God, how much it hurts!" he took her hands and slid them down on his neck to make her feel his heartbeats. "This…what you can feel. I couldn't feel it any more. I wondered why it was still working when all I feeling dead inside."

"Arman…," she began, horrified at the thought.

"I don't know why I left you. I was delirious with 'flu and I couldn't stop thinking about you with another man. I thought it was just pure jealousy; but later I realised it was just plain hypocrisy," he said, giving her a faraway look. "Why did you come here, Ria?"

"I need a father for my baby. I couldn't deny my child of that pleasure. I never had my own father," her breath seemed to come intermingled with tears. "I want you to love our baby," she admitted. "Dad was going crazy with guilt at home and I…missed you."

Arman stopped breathing at her sincerity and touched by her solemn words. But still his heart longed to hear those three words again and this time just for him, "You said you loved me?"

"Yes…I love you," her eyes brimmed and she ignored when tears fell one by one. "I shouldn't, right? You troubled me so much!"

"Oh God.... please don't ever stop loving me even if I act like such a fool!" he said, gathering her around his chest in a tight grip. "You are just good for me. Without you I just feel so empty."

"Me too; I love you so much," Ria said, thinking about Mike for a second and Arman's acute jealousy over the matter. "Stop asking me about my past. You have grilled me enough."

Arman grinned, "I will. There is nothing left I guess. I don't know why I keep digging for dead tigers."

"You just want to hurt yourself, you masochist," she hit him playfully but there was remorse in her voice.

"I just can't think of you being with someone else," he said glumly. Ria didn't respond to that but her face turned pale. She didn't exactly take the statement kindly, "Hey, now don't think I have stopped loving you. I just told you how I feel..."

"Sometimes keep your feelings to yourself," Ria tried to roll away but Arman's hands were quicker and he pulled her hard against himself, "Don't leave me."

Ria sighed deeply, feeling at home in his arms. "I don't want to...perhaps we can just make love and forget..."

"No."

"No?" Ria turned to look at him. "What do you mean by 'no'?"

Arman beamed, "Yes, let's talk."

Ria made a sound as if she would choke. Speculating on his wife's breathing problem, Arman quickly turned over to look at her with his heart in his eyes. She was openly laughing at him now, her eyes shining with unshed tears.

"Are you going to take up that job at the school?" he asked, playing with her curls.

"Yes, it's something I want to do," she hugged him.

"Then you should do it. I'll help you take care of our baby," he added solemnly. He began to kiss her.

"W...what did I do *now*?"

"I love you," Arman said, smiling.

"You want to talk, but I don't."

"Then what do you want to do?" he asked, rolling on his back and staring at her naked glory.

Ria wriggled her eyebrows mirthfully and winked, "What do you think I want to do?"

"My God...you?...Yes! *Yes*!" he laughed as she crawled over him and sealed her lips with his.

* * * * *

Amitab Melhera and his wife were sleeping apart. There was no scope for any sort of conversation and neither of them asked any questions. And when at work, Amitab never grew tired of cursing himself for being such a fool as to put his daughter in such an impossible situation.

"How many nights are we going to sleep this way?"

Vidhya didn't want to answer. Her audible sigh made his heart feel heavy. He didn't deserve a woman like Vidhya, who had been so loving and patient all these years while all he had done was to spoil their daughter's life. He couldn't even handle a daughter. He had been a bad father.

"I'm wondering what could have happened to Ria? It's been three days since she left, but she hasn't called. Do you think she would be alright?"

"I got a call from Jeevan. She reached Arman's office, safely."

"And then what?"

Amitab turned to face his wife, who had tears in her eyes. "Oh God, darling...I'm so sorry! I messed up, didn't I? I thought everything would be perfect...I..."

"Shhh...," she moved towards him and both fell into each other's arms. He held her tightly, almost trembling with remorse. "I agree it was not a perfect plan but it could have been worse..."

"You are just saying this to comfort me..."

"Yes. I'm lying," Vidhya managed to smile. "All I'm thinking about is our daughter. Though she is strong, I feel she becomes weak when it comes to choosing the right person in her life. She could be very happy with Arman...Arman could have been very happy with her...but both are pig-headed...," she took a long breath. "I think we should..."

Just then the phone bell rang and Amitab jumped at the noise it was making. "Who could it be at this hour of the...Ria," he breathed aloud, "*Ria*!" His wife watched him, amused as he picked up the phone and yelled Ria's name again, "Where are you? What are you...doing? Who is that with *you*!?"

Vidhya's ears perked, "What happened?"

Amitab looked red with anger or embarrassment, she couldn't tell. He moved silently and put the phone into the speaker mode.

"Are you trying to tell me that you and Arman are not getting a divorce?"

"Yes, Dad...I..."

"Why? He didn't get hold of a good lawyer or he didn't have a good excuse?" Amitab growled. "How can you tell me that you are not getting a divorce? After all the arguments and tears…"

"Amitab!" Vidhya shook her head. "Do you want our daughter to get a divorce or what? I'll talk to her and you can shut up."

Amitab moved to place the phone out of reach from his wife, "Don't talk like an old-fashioned grandmother…I'm not letting my daughter compromise on anything now!"

"Mom! I'm so sorry I didn't know how to tell you but Arman says he wants the baby and I…"

"The idiot *wants you for the baby?"*

"No Dad! I…"

"You better come back."

"*We* are coming back," they heard Arman's voice vibrating through the line. "I would really like to meet you…," his voice sounded contrite. "Would you mind if we come after a week? I thought Ria and I could spend some time together…"

"I want you here after a week then!" Amitab's voice boomed as he banged down the phone.

Vidhya blinked her eyes, shocked at her husband's response, "Why did you do that?"

"What?"

"Bang the phone down."

"I didn't want them to change their mind," Amitab replied gruffly and met his wife's eyes that were brimming with happiness. "Good they came back to their senses," he said, moving towards her. "And it feels good…." he said, pulling her hard into his arms, with pride and possession, "to get my wife back!"

Epilogue

"It's a girl!"

"Arman, everybody's watching...stop jumping around." An outraged Amitab pulled him to a corner.

Beaming at his father-in-law, Arman shrugged helplessly, "I'm so happy...I want to jump!"

Everybody was happy. Amitab couldn't contain himself with happiness which had knocked on their door too late or rather too leisurely. He walked towards their door. Time tested them all. He was glad that they all had emerged winners. Ria and Arman, after settling down in New York, had made it clear that they were planning to bring up the baby there. Vidhya, on the other hand, wanted them to stay back in India as she wanted to help with the baby. Amitab was glad but wondered if it was the right thing to do because after all, his daughter was still a baby! How could she manage all alone?

"Don't you want to look at your grandchild?"

"Of course I do!" Amitab asserted joyfully. He was quietly excited.

"It's my turn to hold the baby," Arman declared and ran towards Ria's room. Both the men almost reached at the same time but none could hold the baby.

"Not now. We need to clean her first," said the grumpy nurse, taking the baby away from the room.

Arman almost felt like sticking his tongue out at her. He turned to look at Ria and found her sound asleep. There was a smile on her lips that played peacefully for a long time. Watching her, he could hardly contain his happiness. He had everything in his life now – a beautiful wife and now a beautiful daughter.

He would see her grow up into a beautiful woman who would share her life with them. The prospect of raising the little one delighted him so much that he almost made it out of the room to take a look at her.

"What shall we name her?"

"It would be an Indian name," Vidhya said forcefully and the look in her eyes conveyed that she would brook no argument.

"She will be living here…an Indian name would be difficult to pronounce!" Amitab sulked. He went ahead and made himself comfortable on the sofa that was placed in front of the bed.

Looking around, one couldn't tell if it was a hospital room or a hotel room. It was very well designed and furnished, Amitab admitted to himself. Arman had been visiting the hospital for a week to check if everything had been arranged beforehand.

"I don't mind an Indian name," Arman professed generously to his worried mother-in-law. "I was wondering why Dad isn't here?"

The door opened and Jeevan came in, but what he had in his hands surprised them all. The little girl was awake and gurgling with a curious look on her face.

"See, how beautiful she is."

"Hey, I was going to hold her first!" Amitab stood up, almost offended.

"Ha! You are too late," grinned a contented Jeevan, lulling her slowly to sleep.

"What is all this noise?" Ria opened her eyes, almost exhausted out of her wits. She couldn't remember the last time when she had felt so happy or was it in Arman's arms? Of late he had been cuddling her so much that she had to tell him that she couldn't take all the pampering. But secretly she had to admit that she loved it. She had assumed her father to be the best husband in the world, but Arman outshone everyone in that department. Not that she could say it aloud, but coming all the way and telling Arman that she loved him had been worth all the trouble that she had taken.

Just then Arman looked at her and all the love in the world was right there in his eyes for everyone to see.

"What shall we name her?" he asked her softly, taking her hands in hers.

He didn't sport the long hair any more. She had been disappointed with his decision to shorten his hair but he had firmly said that he wouldn't want his daughter to be scared when she played with him. In any case, Arman looked a lot more handsome and younger now. With his short hair and glasses, his grey eyes seemed to twinkle all the time. He looked so happy.

"I want you to name her," she whispered.

"How about Maliha…?"

"What does that mean?"

"*Beautiful…strong…*," Arman enunciated and Jeevan put the baby in his arms. He lifted the exquisite gift in his palms and raised her to the heavens. The little baby made uncomfortable noises and they all smiled indulgently. "She will be beautiful because it's in her genes...." making everybody laugh. He continued, "But she would be strong because that is the kind of person she deserves to be..." He regarded Ria with love and respect as he added, "...just like her mother."

All eyes turned to him, wondering how love could change people so much.

"She is going to break some hearts," Amitab sighed as if dreading that day.

"Dad, I hope there will be no matchmaking from your side now," Ria literally growled at her father.

"That was...*different*," he concluded lamely. "But we learn from our mistakes...." When everybody looked sceptical about his statement, he gave in willingly, "My mistakes, I mean."

Arman almost felt sorry for his father-in-law for becoming the target of all.

"Don't worry, nothing of the sort is going to happen. We will find her a rich handsome guy who will buy the world for her."

The women in the room now glared at Arman.

"As if, I'll let you!" Ria said, laughing and pursing her lips at the same time. "You think only rich people can fall in love with rich people?"

"I...I'm not saying that, but..."

"*Shoo*...all of you...go out. I'm tired with all this drama. I'm off to sleep," she said, closing her eyes and sighing contentedly.

Arman felt like a rogue then as his wife had been through a tough time bearing him the most wonderful thing he could ever want and he was already upsetting her.

"I'll take care of her," he whispered softly in his wife's ears.

The rest of them left the room but Arman stayed on, looking at her. Without makeup, she always looked so vulnerable. Who could have said that Ria was already a mother?

"I'm sorry Ria..."

"It's okay, Arman...," she opened her eyes and smiled. "Now come here and thank me for the baby I gave you."

"Oh God, I love you!" Arman said, wanting to cradle her in his arms but since he couldn't, he bent and kissed her hard on her lips. They felt softer than satin and smoother than pearls.

"And I love you. Don't get me wrong. I love being married to you but with you around, I'm always on my edge," she winked.

"I wouldn't have met you then," Arman said, his voice softening as it alighted on her tired face. "But you know that I'll love you forever...that's a promise."

"I know...that's a promise," she closed her eyes again and this time sleep caved her in. It was a beautiful world – not perfect but enough to keep her happy. At that moment, the only thing that kept lingering in her mind was Arman's words coupled with the warmth of his love.

She heard a cooing Maliha around her and thought about waking up but Arman jumped and picked her up. The little one looked delighted to be in his arms, just as she had been and would always be...always.

Legally, Lovingly Yours

By Abhishek Bose

Price	:	Rs. 125
Pages	:	186
Size	:	5.0×7.75 inches
Binding	:	Paperback
Language	:	English
Subject	:	Fiction/Romance
ISBN	:	9788183520195

About the book:

Love-hate-jealousy-admiration-amity-animosity-friendship-enmity—for people in general may be only words, but for eighteen-year old Abhishek Banerjee these words turned out to be life-changing experiences over the next five years.

He harboured dreams of studying in a good college, to make new friends there, to have a girl by his side as his girlfriend, and above all, to carve out a niche for himself and leave his mark. He started realising his dreams when he got selected to study in the Animus Law School, one of the premier private law schools of the country. But, on the very first day he realised that Lady Luck was not on his side.

Could he make new friends as he had yearned for? Did he meet and get the girl he dreamt of? Was he able to make his mark? If no, then why not? If yes, then how?

Blessed with a nature endowed with patience, helpful attitude, desire for friendship, a never-say-die spirit and a never-give-in attitude, Abhishek embarks on a five-year long journey through college and on the way faces all kinds of experiences, both good and bad.

Let's Get Committed

By Smita Kaushik and Utkarsh Roy

Price	:	Rs. 125
Pages	:	240
Size	:	5.0×7.75 inches
Binding	:	Paperback
Language	:	English
Subject	:	Fiction/Romance
ISBN	:	9788183520157

About the book:

Hierarchy of modern age love:

Orkut > Chatting > Phone > CCD > Movies

Apurv and Radhika get committed. They try to adjust to their new marital status committed by proving the equation 1+1=1.

- Facebook status = In a relationship…Orkut status: committed.

- In a given area, low population density implies hands together & lesser, lips and cheeks.

- 1st testimonial from him/her…scrapbook full of sweetheart/love.

- Desktop wallpaper = "C:\my pictures\my.sweetheart.jpg"

This stage relates to the fact that even after liking each other, they just experiment with the concept of being together and not because of love…just in hope that they might (if it's written) fall in it.

Being a hottie, Radhika initially misses the single tag and the direct and indirect benefits associated with it. Apurv tries to reinstate the feeling of love in her but fails…though partially…

Life goes on as time tests their compatibility and then suddenly destiny shows its darker side…

Radhika is gone…

What happens next….

If it's love, will it cease to exist if they are apart?

Does Apurv find a new love?

Rs 199/-

Rs 199/-

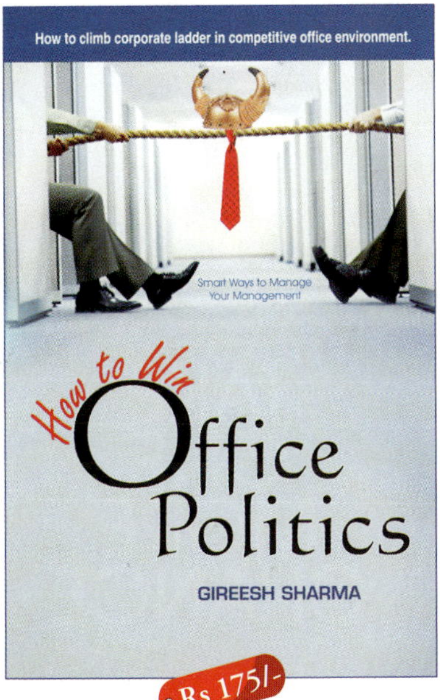

Rs 175/-

Rs 149/-

The Most Eligible Bachelor
Life Beyond Thinking
Satyapal Chandra
Rs 125/-

Let's Get Committed...
Love will follow... maybe...
Passion
Friendship
Status Symbol
Smita Kaushik
Utkarsh Roy
Rs 125/-

Abhishek Bose
Legally, Lovingly Yours
Rs 125/-

Shriya Garg
TAKE ONE MORE CHANCE
A satire comedy by a sixteen-year old
Rs 125/-

The Promise
How far would you go for the one you love?
Chital Mehta
Rs 125/-

Beyond Love
What lies beneath?
Ankit Uttam
Rs 125/-

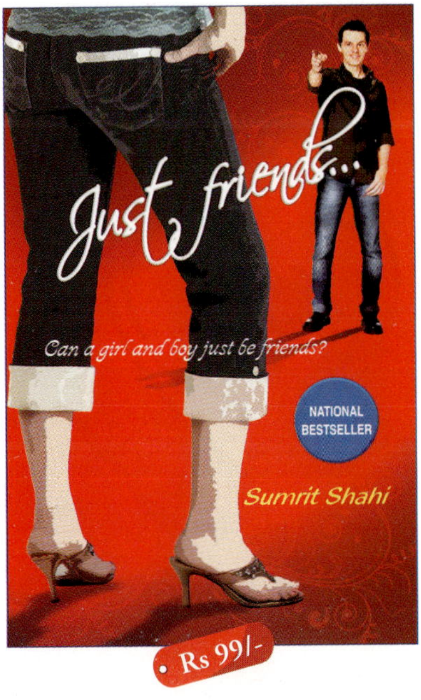
Just friends...
Can a girl and boy just be friends?
NATIONAL BESTSELLER
Sumrit Shahi
Rs 99/-

Love
Life and Ambition
Give your name an identity
Bharat Agarwal
Rs 99/-

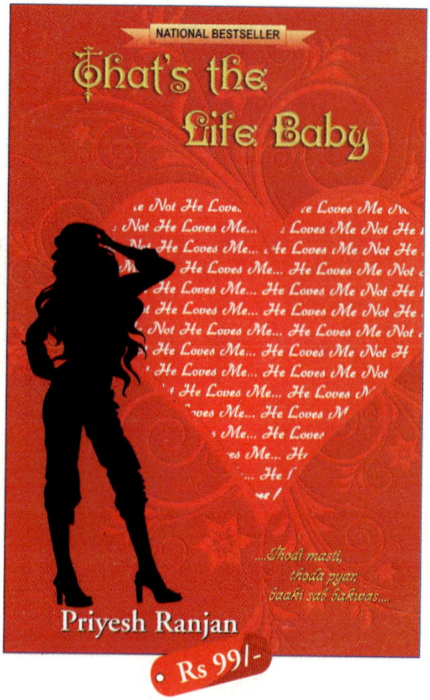
NATIONAL BESTSELLER
That's the Life Baby
...Thodi masti, thoda pyar, baaki sab bakwas...
Priyesh Ranjan
Rs 99/-

the saga of love
via telephone
Pankaj Pandey
Rs 99/-

She turned I saw her turning
The true love never dies...
MUSHTAQ AHMAD & NABI NAZEER
Rs 99/-

Love Guru
More than 1,000 tips on the mysteries of love and success
I Love you
MK Mazumdar
Rs 125/-